Advance Praise

It was a dark and stormy night... (You don't get to say that often living here in Los Angeles, but on February 27, 2014 -- it was, indeed, a dark and stormy night. Go ahead, Google it.) And while part of me was thinking "I hope it rains enough to help us out with this drought," the rest of me was thinking -- what a perfect night to sit down and read *Bill of Frights*, by The League of Eclectic Authors.

I have to say, I enjoyed the hell out of this book, and the many soon-to-be-going-to/recently-arrived-from Hell denizens in its fantastic, brisk, and creepy stories. When it's at its best, I felt like I was 14 years old again, reading that great Stephen King collection, *Night Shift*. Especially the stories like *The Bunny Man Returns*, and *Shadows in Georgetown*. *The Bunny Man* is a fun twist on those great old Urban Legends of a serial killer who's STANDING RIGHT BEHIND YOU. I loved it. I didn't see the end coming, and enjoyed every twist in the road getting there. Very much like a tragic car accident you don't see coming, I suppose. And *Shadows in Georgetown* -- what a creepy tale, with even more sinister implications. I truly hope Donald Jeffries writes more about those Shadows -- I want to know more. *The Last Post* is a great ghost story. Like most good ghost stories, I can't really say too much about it without spoiling some surprises, but having grown up in the shadow of a Civil War battlefield, Stones River, this one hit pretty close to home for me. It reminded me a lot of the tales I heard around the fire growing up. *The Bargain* was a perfect way to start the book off -- it felt like a cool little *Twilight Zone* -- clever, sexy, and truly horrible. And the *Caretaker* felt like I'd taken a little too much acid, gone into a fun-house, and wandered into a room I wasn't supposed to see. And I mean that in a good way (how else could I mean it?). *Bill of Frights* is a perfect addition to the creepy section of your short story shelf. And when a good thunderstorm hits, pour yourself a little scotch, turn on the gas fire, and dig in.

-Robert Ben Garant, screenwriter, *Night at the Museum*

Is there something about D.C. that brings out the murderous psychopath in all of us? Read this marvelous anthology and you can be the judge. In *Bill of Frights* you have 14 stories of horror, science fiction, paranormal, fantasy and speculative fiction, all tied in some wicked, wonderful way to the Washington area. From the region's own urban legend in *The Bunny Man Returns,* to the political dystopian tale *Farewell Washington,* to a ghostly sighting in the Air and Space museum in *History Lesson, Bill of Frights* proves that whether it's love, death, war, or politics, everything is different in D.C..

-- Alma Katsu, author of the acclaimed *Taker* Trilogy

Bill of Frights

The League of
Eclectic Authors

Pocol Press
Clifton, VA

POCOL PRESS
Published in the United States of America
by Pocol Press
6023 Pocol Drive
Clifton, VA 20124
www.pocolpress.com

Publisher's Cataloguing-in-Publication

The League of Eclectic Authors
    Bill of frights / The League of Eclectic Authors.
    p. cm.
    ISBN: 978-1-929763-57-3
1. Horror stories. 2. Short stories, American --Washington (D.C.)
3. Washington (D.C.) --Fiction. 4. Ghosts--Fiction. 5. Urban
folklore --United States.   I. Title.

        PS3612.E212 B55 2014

    813.6–dc23   2014933366

Library of Congress Control Number: 2014933366

Cover photo by Traci Crawford.

Graphic assistance by Amelia Hetrick.

About the Group

In 2011, two Washington, D.C.-based authors; Clint Mesle and Clint Collins (yes, these are their real names) wanted to create a support group for local genre writers to meet to critique and discuss their work and to encourage local writers in all stages of creation. The first couple of meetings were held in the conference room of a local New Age store—which seemed to fit as many of the writers of the new group specialized in horror and fantasy fiction. Soon, word of mouth spread and membership grew to over thirty strong, with writers from all genres including sci-fi, fantasy, horror, thriller, historical, and nonfiction. The group encourages all writers as it currently boasts fiction and nonfiction authors, a folklorist, screenwriters, poets, and even a multi-media television personality in its ranks. Please enjoy this first anthology as there is much more to come. Welcome to The League of Eclectic Authors!

Table of Contents

The Bargain
Clint Collins

"*That* was good," said the demon, finishing off the last of her pisco sour, a tongue a little longer and redder than normal swirling around the bottom of the glass. "I'll have another."

Diego, a Chilean from Santiago, knew just how to make a memorable one. It was his trademark drink at "El Orinoco," a Georgetown restaurant famous for its excellent and authentic South American cuisine.

The demon tossed back long blonde hair and leaned upon the gleaming bar of exotic wood found only in the deepest reaches of the Amazon, a sulfurous perfume exhaling from her cleavage. With eyes that could never hold a shade of blue, always reverting to a diabolical yellow, she turned to see the last of the dinner crowd leaving. The satrap for seduction in the District of Columbia, chosen by Asmodeus himself, smelled lust in the air and her painted toes curled in their black six-inch heels. Swiveling, her hot golden eyes met Diego's.

"So, tell me about your little schoolgirl."

Diego smiled. "Miranda is hardly a schoolgirl. She's a senior at Catholic University." Squinting, he put the demon's second and slightly stronger pisco sour before her. "Majoring, I think, in international business. At least that's what she told me." Diego had given her a couple free drinks on her twenty-first birthday and he remembered every word of their brief conversation. She was Brazilian, from Sao Paulo, with rain forest-green eyes and flowing black hair like a waterfall at midnight.

It really hadn't been all that hard contacting a demon. A lapsed Catholic, Diego did try prayer at first, even going to mass at St. Patrick's, pleading for a single night with her in exchange for a complete conversion. After a few months he still got no more than a polite smile from Miranda as she headed to her favorite table with her friends, although there were more lingering ones from the new hostess, a pretty Venezuelan with a cross of gold around her neck.

1

But he wanted to hear Miranda's sighs and feel those warm red lips pressed to his. Sometimes he woke at night with pounding heart, still feeling the dream in which she was tightly wound about him like a smooth-hipped python, squeezing the breath from him. The desire was just as crushing and he found himself walking out of an occult bookstore one day clutching a black-leather grimoire seething with black magic recipes to satisfy almost any hunger.

The demon, anxious to arrange yet another senatorial seduction of an intern in a few hours, folded manicured hands and got to the point. "And so, you wish to be with her for a single night? Easy enough. Are the terms acceptable?"

Diego did not hesitate. "Yes, they are acceptable. A year off my life?"

The demon took a sip, then shook her head. "A common misunderstanding. It is a year of service to His Infernal Majesty we desire, not the abbreviation of your existence."

The bartender frowned. "Service? What do I have to do?"

"Just a few favors. Nothing all that risky, don't worry." She opened her purse, stitched from the skin of a priest who forgot certain key words and failed to exorcise her from a Spanish girl in the 1920s, and spread a piece of parchment over the bar. Steam rose like delivered souls as the paper found moisture on the counter.

The demon spun the document toward him. "Sign here for one night with Miranda Raquel Cabral within sunset to sunrise, date and time to be determined, but within the calendar year of servitude to His Infernal Majesty and/or His duly designated representatives." She offered a straight pin. "In blood, of course."

Later, the demon pushed a phone number to him. "Call this in fifteen minutes. Ask for Sue, then hang up."

Over the next few months, Diego made drinks weaker or stronger as required, secretly canceled or made reservations, gave the demon hairs from the heads of the most attractive waitresses…and waited.

His cell phone vibrated in his pocket on a slow and moonless November night and he left the bar without a word, driving to the D.C. morgue on Massachusetts Avenue. The demon gave exact instructions. Certain doors would be unlocked and certain hallways and desks would be vacant.

Miranda lay still on the gurney, white sheet cresting over the full bosom that caught his gaze so many times at "El Orinoco." The only visible sign of some fatal imperfection was a dull purpling on the side of her neck.

"I'm sorry," said the demon, this time an old man in a stained lab coat. "She was biking with friends on the C&O canal. Somehow...she fell." Its eyes had lost some of their glow, as if even a creature of Hell could be touched by the loss of someone so young and beautiful.

For the first time ever, Diego touched her hand, fingers interlacing with slender, cooler ones. He turned to the demon. "Did you know this would happen?"

The old man shook his head. "No, we did not foresee this." He sighed. "Are we not all subject to God's will?"

Unable to resist, Diego ran a hand through glossy black hair draping over the gurney's edge like a black flag.

The demon cleared its throat. "Per our contract, you have until sunrise. People will start showing up after that and you don't want to be found here." The demon paused. This was its favorite part. The fine print. "Just so you know, you still owe us six months and twelve days."

"What?" Diego motioned to the body beside him. "Look at her. She's *dead*. Doesn't that break the deal?"

Now it was a security guard with a heavy flashlight. "We never promised you she'd be alive. Only that you get a night with her. Read the contract." It held the door open a sliver before leaving Diego with his cold and lovely prize. "I'll be in touch."

Walking down the hallway, heading toward the garage where it would unlock three doors to facilitate a massive car theft, the demon smiled wearily. These mortals would never learn.

The devil is *always* in the details.

The Bunny Man Returns
Clint Mesle

"And it was on a night, just like this, where two young stoners were getting high in their car, when suddenly, one of them looks in the rear view mirror and screams out 'Oh, my God! He's going to kill us!' and that's when the axe came crashing through the back window....KAR-RASH! When the stoners tried to start the car and get away, the man with the axe had already slashed the tires down to the rims. KAR-RASH! The front windshield is smashed. Then the scared high school pothead looks up and sees the six-foot tall axeman standing over them. The axeman wearing a white bunny suit."

"Wait a minute," Heather Kunkle cuts in. "A bunny suit?"

"Let me finish," Jimmy Diaz said as he touched Heather's lips with his forefinger. "The two stoners had come face to face with the notorious Bunny Man of Guinea Road."

"That is, without a doubt, the lamest story I've ever heard. That was supposed to be scary? A guy dressed up like Peter Cottontail? A demented Easter Bunny? You can do better than that, Jimmy."

"Ah, but would you say that if you knew the story was true?" Jimmy shot back.

"The Bunny Man is an urban legend. Something our parents told us so we would get home before dark. It's always a guy with an axe or a hook in a bunny suit. It's all a bunch of crap and you know it."

"All urban legends start in fact. There is always a thread of truth running through them. You do believe me, don't you?"

On the last line Jimmy moved in for a kiss. They were sitting close together in the front seat of Jimmy's beat-up Toyota pickup truck. Heather met him halfway but made sure the kiss wasn't passionate. She had only known Jimmy for two months' and this was only their second date. She didn't know how serious she could get over a boy whose license plate read KILLA. She never dated anyone seriously and wanted to enjoy her last year of high school without any serious attachments. Besides, she knew her father wasn't too crazy about Jimmy because, well, for

4

many reasons, but most of them were the color of his skin and his wild California attitude.

"Stop it. My dad could be watching," Heather said as she pulled back.

"Is he home? I want to talk to him."

Heather was taken aback.

"Why would you want to talk to my dad?"

"Duh! Haven't you been listening? The Bunny Man sighting. The last one was in 1977. Your old man was one of the teenagers that saw him that night. His name was listed as a witness in *The Washington Post* article from 1977. He saw the Bunny Man!"

"Oh, I see," Heather started, a little hurt. "You only want to date me because you think my father saw the Bunny Man when he was a teenager. You really know how to hurt a girl."

Jimmy smiled. He pulled Heather close to him and tenderly laid his head on her shoulder. He then pulled his sleeve up to show her a tattoo on his arm.

"See my tat? Born to write horror. I want to be a horror writer. It's all I ever wanted to do. My old man is in the military and we move around every two or three years. Whenever we move to a new town I do my research on any supernatural events and this place, Fairfax, Virginia, is a freaky hotbed of supernatural activity—Civil War ghosts, alien sightings, and the biggest story of all—the Bunny Man murder of 1977. But here is the kick-ass part of the story. There've been Bunny Man sightings in Fairfax dating back to 1865! Your old man is the last living witness to have seen the Bunny Man. You gotta let me talk to him."

Still hurt, Heather pushed Jimmy away.

"I see. You only want to date me because you think my dad saw some dork in a bunny suit back in the seventies? You're an asshole, Jimmy."

"Hey, I didn't know you were Henry Kunkle's daughter until after I met you. Now come over here and kiss me."

She obeyed and leaned in for a long kiss. She realized that she was starting to have feelings for this boy from California. But a quick glance in Jimmy's rearview mirror made her jump away from Jimmy.

"Oh God. It's my father. He's watching us."

Henry Kunkle was standing behind Jimmy's pick-up truck watching them through the back window. To Heather's surprise, Jimmy jumped out of the truck to where Kunkle was standing. Heather followed quickly behind.

"Mr. Kunkle. Jimmy Diaz. Damn glad to meet you."

Jimmy extended his hand to shake. Kunkle just stood there and stared at him. Heather finally broke the silence.

"Daddy, this is my friend Jimmy Diaz. He's from Los Angeles. He's a boy in my high school. He wants to be a writer."

It seemed like an eternity before Mr. Kunkle finally shook Jimmy's hand.

"Mister....Diaz was it? Do me a favor and don't park in front of my driveway next time. Your truck is something of an eyesore. I don't want my neighbors.....talking. Come along, Heather. Supper is on the table."

Kunkle grabbed his daughter's arm and pulled her away from Jimmy. As they started to walk away, Jimmy followed quickly behind.

"Mr. Kunkle, I wonder if I can interview you about the Bunny Man sighting back in 1977? I understand you were a witness to the murder?"

Kunkle stopped half-way up his driveway. He pushed Heather forward towards the front door and turned around and faced Jimmy.

"There is no such thing as the Bunny Man, Mr. Diaz. I've been telling people that for thirty-some years. Have a good evening."

"But *The Washington Post* lists you by name. You gonna tell me the whole news story was bullshit?"

"Good night, Mr. Diaz."

Once inside his house, Kunkle locked his front door and looked out the peephole. Jimmy finally got into his pick-up truck and drove away.

"Unusual looking boy. What is his background?" Kunkle asked his daughter.

"His father is Mexican-American and his mother is Korean. Why?"

"A true American mutt. I don't like him. Besides being rude he asks too many questions. You're not seriously going out with this boy, are you?"

"You're such a racist, daddy! Yes, I am dating him. What are you going to do? Lock me in my room and forbid me to see him?"

"Of course not. Because that would make you want to date him even more. You will get sick of him, eventually. Girls like you usually do."

"What the fuck does that mean?"

"Language!" Kunkle yelled. He reached over and grabbed his daughter and shook her.

"Listen, I don't care if he's from Mars and has green skin and four balls. I don't want you seeing that boy. He asks too many damned questions. I will not let some punk kid open up old wounds and drag our name through the mud again. Do you understand?"

Heather weakly nodded back a yes.

"You have never told me about that night, daddy. Did you really see....something that night?"

"Teenagers, drugs and beer. That's what happened that night. Your mind plays tricks on you when you're stoned. And that's all it was. Some people get drunk and see pink elephants.

"Some people see men dressed in bunny suits. Let that be a lesson to you, young lady. Don't do drugs. Now how about we order a pizza for dinner?"

31 OCTOBER 2:30 PM

Henry Kunkle was just about finished raking leaves in his front yard when he noticed Jimmy Diaz sitting in the cab of his truck watching him from a distance. Kunkle pretended he wasn't there, but just as Kunkle closed the last leaf bag, Jimmy came out of his truck and stood three feet away from Kunkle. Finally, Kunkle turned and faced him.

"Something I can help you with, son?"

"Why? Why won't you talk to me? You need to set the record straight on what you saw that night."

7

"I don't owe you nothing. Give it a rest, boy. A boy committed suicide that night. Split his head open when he got stoned, climbed a tree, and dove off thinking he could fly like Superman. He couldn't. End of story."

"*The Washington Post* didn't see it that way. There were eyewitnesses that swear the boy was attacked by a man in a bunny suit and his head was split open with an axe. The boy that was killed, Donnie Wheelock, was a friend of yours, wasn't he?"

Donnie Wheelock. Kunkle had not heard that name in years. In high school they were thick as thieves. It was Donnie who first introduced Kunkle to pot one afternoon in Donnie's basement. They shared their first joint while watching Droopy cartoons. Every time Droopy spoke in his monotone twang the two boys would erupt with laughter. Before they knew it they would spent every afternoon hanging out together getting stoned and watching cartoons after school. When they didn't have pocket change for pot, Donnie would raid his parents' liquor cabinet. By the time they reached the twelfth grade, they were complete stoners and proud of it.

"It happened over there. Under the streetlight in front of your house," Jimmy pointed. "There was a Halloween party going on in your house that was getting out of control. Kids were streaming out of your house and overflowing onto your lawn and street. You and Donnie Wheelock, very drunk and stoned, were getting ready to go on another beer run when the Bunny Man appeared out of the woods over there. Donnie never even saw it coming. The axe came down on his head and killed him instantly. Drunk teenagers on your lawn saw the Bunny Man and screamed and pointed but the man in the white bunny suit quickly disappeared into the woods on the other side of the street. A number of witnesses say that you just stood there and watched it all. That you were five feet away from the Bunny Man and you did nothing. Just stood there as he played Paul Bunyan on your best friend's head. You stood face to face with a murderer and did nothing to help your friend. Why was that, Mr. Kunkle?"

Kunkle paused. Then finally spoke:

"You want the truth, Mr. Diaz? I was so stoned that night I thought I was having hallucinations. I've seen worse things than

8

giant bunnies when I was stoned. There was no Bunny Man. There never was. Just a bunch of stoned kids seeing things. Now please just leave me and my family alone."

"I don't believe you. You're lying," Jimmy shot back, unafraid.

"Dammit, boy. What is your problem? Why do you care? You writing a book or something?"

"As a matter of fact," Jimmy smiled. "I am."

HALLOWEEN NIGHT. 7:30 PM

"Come out. I want to see you," Jimmy screamed from outside Heather's window.

Heather was still in her bedroom looking over her Halloween costume. Against her wishes, Jimmy wanted her to dress up as a Playboy bunny. The outfit was cute, though a tad revealing, and Heather wished she had dropped the ten pounds she wanted to drop over the summer. She figured it was cold enough outside that she could wear a jacket and cover up most of the outfit. The fishnet stockings were a little tight, and the black high heels were killing her feet. She actually liked the bunny ears. She made sure to bend the wire just so to make one ear droopy, just like the magazine cover. She took one final look at herself in the mirror, blew an imaginary kiss at the cute little bunny girl staring back at her, and grabbed her coat.

Heather carefully tiptoed down the staircase. She noticed her father was sleeping in his easy chair in the living room, a copy of Field and Stream laying across his chest. She made her escape through the kitchen door to meet Jimmy outside.

"Oh, babe. You're not gonna wear that coat all night, are you?" was the first thing Jimmy said as she closed the door.

"I'm not freezing my ass off so all of your friends can have a sneak peek at my goods, Jimmy. And what's the deal with your costume? You're going as some lame-ass clown? Let me guess, Krusty or Bozo?"

"Are you kidding me? I'm John Wayne Gacy. You know, the serial killer that raped and killed 33 boys between 1972 and 1978. Isn't it obvious?"

"That is really gross. And why am I dating you again?"

9

"Because you love sexy, dirty clowns and hot, nasty clown sex."

Jimmy grabbed Heather and kissed her. Heather was seriously starting to wonder if this relationship was a mistake. Jimmy's hands were trying to find a way under her jacket. Heather playfully pushed him away.

"Calm down, John Wayne. We have a party to go to, remember?"

Heather was promised a costume party with food and drinks. What she got was Jimmy and twelve of his friends drinking cheap beer and jumping around on some poor parents' couch. She felt uncomfortable and never took off her jacket. It was getting close to her curfew and she wanted to go home. Jimmy continued drinking and dancing to some loud rap song. Finally, Heather gave up and just left the party without saying goodbye. As she walked out the door, she was now convinced that her relationship with Jimmy was over.

She took a shortcut through Echofall Woods. The woods had a walking trail but it was almost impossible to see in the dark. The moonlight over her head helped, but she still twisted her ankle when her foot missed the asphalt trail and hit the dirt and gravel. She cursed as she took off her high heels and threw them into the woods.

She was in no rush to get home. After all, it was Halloween night.

She loved Echofall Woods ever since she was a child and wasn't afraid of the stories of Civil War ghosts that were supposed to haunt the woods. She was amazed that it was Halloween and she was alone in Echofall. Usually on Halloween night brave little kids in superhero costumes summed up the courage to run up and down the trail on a Halloween candy sugar high looking for ghosts. Or teenage assholes hiding in the woods trying to scare the kids.

In the distance Heather could see the lights from her back porch. She was almost home. She checked her watch: 11:20. She made her curfew. Yes!

The trail ended and she was now walking through the woods towards her house. She tried to keep the branches from hitting her face as she pushed forward towards her house. Then,

10

she got that feeling. That feeling they always get in the movies when they know they are not alone.

She stopped and turned around, half expecting to find a group of kids in costumes ready to attack her with water balloons. It took a second or two for her eyes to focus in the dark but there was no mistaking it. Standing before her was a man dressed in a white bunny suit. The man in the bunny suit was too far away for Heather to see his (or her) face, and the mysterious figure was content just to stand there staring at Heather. Heather was a little scared but wasn't freaking out. The big bunny suit was comical. It reminded her of Ralphie's pink bunny suit from *A Christmas Story*.

"Is that you, Ralphie? Did you get your Red Ryder BB gun for Christmas?" Heather mocked. The big bunny didn't make a sound. Now she was getting a little freaked out.

Heather was ready to turn and run but suddenly the big bunny figure spoke:

"I like your ears."

Heather didn't recognize the voice. It was young. Male. Monotone.

"Thanks," Heather returned. "I like yours, too. I just left a lame costume party. I guess you were at one, too."

No answer. Now she was scared. She slowly began to make her escape.

"Okay. Bye Mr. Bunny man. This little bunny has to hop, hop, hop back home. My father is probably waiting for me on the porch with a shotgun on his lap. My father loves guns. Loves to shoot them, too. You have a good night now."

The Bunny Man was hiding something behind his back. He lifted his axe and showed it off proudly in the moonlight. He then pointed the axe at Heather.

"I am going to kill you, Heather Kunkle."

That's all she needed to hear. She turned and ran towards the safety of her house, never once looking back behind her.

Heather ran up to her porch and threw the front door, locking it frantically behind her. The sudden emotion of the situation had finally caught up to her as she leaned against the locked door and began to sob. She couldn't understand where her father was, as on any other Halloween night he would be sitting on the front porch with a shotgun on his lap ready to chase away any kids with water balloons and toilet paper.

"Daddy, where are you? Are you home?" she screamed.

Silence.

The metal blade of the axe crashed through the windowpane next to the door. Heather screamed as she jumped up and ran towards the staircase. She ran up the stairs three steps at a time until she reached the safety of her bedroom. She slammed the door, locked it, then started to look for her cellphone. She panicked when she realized she had left her cell in Jimmy's truck.

"Heather, are you in there?" came a voice from the other side of the door.

"Daddy?" Heather shot back, confused.

"Of course it's me. What's going on? Why is your door locked? Open the door, sweetheart."

She hesitated. The soothing voice of her father couldn't erase the questions in her mind.

"Honey, please open your door. You're worrying me. Did that Diaz boy do something to you?"

"No, go away! I don't trust you."

"Trust me? Honey, what are you talking about? It's obvious you're upset about something. Open the door and let's talk."

"Daddy, didn't you see what happened to the door? There's someone in the house. Don't you understand there is a maniac in the house!"

"There is no one here. I can assure you. Now please, open the door."

She wanted to believe him. Slowly, and very carefully, she unlocked the door and opened it half an inch. Her father was standing there, without a bunny suit or an axe in his hands. She threw open the door and hugged him.

"That's my girl. Now, are you going to tell me what's the matter? You must have been upset when you came home because there is broken glass all over the floor. Tell me what happened. If that Diaz boy hurt you, I swear I will break his neck."

Heather pulled back. Over her father's shoulder she saw him again. She wanted to scream but the sound froze in her throat. The sudden shocked look on his daughter's face made Henry turn and look over his shoulder. Three feet behind him stood a six foot man in a rabbit suit holding an axe.

Henry's first reaction was to protect his daughter. He threw himself at the stranger but the axe-wielding Bunny Man was faster. He hit Henry in the stomach with the handle of the axe and Henry fell to his knees, the wind knocked out of him. Heather threw her body over her fallen father's body and sobbed hysterically. The Bunny Man stood over him and lifted his axe for the final death blow. Heather closed her eyes and accepted her fate.

"Ha-ha-ha-ha-ha-ha-ha! I got you good, old man. Psyche!"

Jimmy pulled off his Bunny Man hood, still laughing. His hair was matted with sweat and his white clown make-up was smeared and streaked with sweat. Jimmy has having a hard time catching his breath between his laughter.

"Busted! I got you good. Don't worry about the window. I'll pay for it. It was so worth it to see the look on your faces. That's right, old man. You got it in spades. Now you know how Donnie Wheelock felt just before he died. Maybe now you will talk to me and tell me your Bunny Man story. Hey, I'm talking to you, old man."

Heather couldn't understand why her father wasn't answering Jimmy's taunts. Her fear finally turned to anger as she jumped up and threw herself on Jimmy, scratching his white chalky face with her nails. She cut Jimmy on the cheek, which finally made him stop laughing. Without even thinking, he punched her, hard. Heather tumbled backwards and tripped over her fallen father, knocking her out cold. Angry, Henry finally stood up.

"Crazy bitch. Did you see what she did to my face?"

Henry moved forward. Jimmy picked up the axe and pointed it at Henry's chest.

"Don't go crazy on me, old man. You could have dodged this whole scene if you just told me the truth about the Bunny Man. Now, am I going to get my story or what?"

13

Henry smiled.

"You're right, Jimmy. This is all my fault. I should have told you the whole story from the very beginning. I know that now. But it's not too late. You still want to hear the whole story of the Bunny Man of Fairfax?"

"Hell yeah! I want it! I want the whole story and don't leave out a Goddamned thing!"

"Come with me. I will show you."

Confused, Jimmy followed Henry down the hallway.

"No tricks, old man. I still have the axe."

"That you do, Jimmy. No tricks. Just the truth. Follow me."

Jimmy followed Henry as he pulled down the chain that led to the attic door in the ceiling. The folding ladder slid down and Henry began to climb up. Jimmy followed close behind up the ladder into the attic.

The two entered the attic. The room smelled of dust and old newspapers. There was no light except for a tiny sliver of moonlight coming in from a circular window over their heads. Henry pulled on a chain and the room was bathed in electric light. It took a while for Jimmy's eyes to adjust to the light but once they did, he dropped his axe in shock.

At first Jimmy thought he was now in a museum, or a shrine. One the walls around them were axes of all different shapes and sizes. They were surrounded by four or five different mannequins, all dressed in Bunny Man costumes. All of the costumes were crude and homemade, made of cloth, leather and even metal. One of the bunny suits was black. Another was simply a white hood with sewn on bunny ears over what seemed to Jimmy was a confederate civil war uniform.

The walls were covered with newspaper clippings and black and white photos. The first clipping that Jimmy read was from 1907. One of the black and white photos was of a man on a horse. Both the man and the horse were wearing bunny man hoods.

Jimmy's mind was swimming. He nervously picked up his axe again and backed away from Henry.

"You're the Bunny Man!"

14

"Well, no. Not really. You see, Jimmy. When your family lives in a town as long as my family has lived in Fairfax you see a lot of changes. After the Civil War when my great-grandfather came back from fighting alongside General Lee, some carpetbagging son of a bitch told him that his land was no longer his, and he had to get off his land or face the hangman's noose. Well, my great-granddaddy didn't take to his threat very well and let's just say that carpetbagger's neck grew a foot longer that night. It was the war and the plague of reconstruction that gave birth to the first Bunny Man. And ever since then the Bunny Man would rise up and pick up the mantle of my great granddaddy to right a great wrong."

"You killed the Wheelock boy!" Jimmy screamed.

"No, actually it was my dear father that killed Donnie Wheelock. You have to understand that Donnie was leading me down a desperate path of drugs and alcohol. I probably would have died of an overdose if my daddy's blade didn't end Donnie's life that night. No great loss. Even his parents didn't like him. Everyone in town knew Donnie was a drug addict and a thief so it was no shock to hear that he took a bad trip and died."

"You sick inbred redneck. I'm gonna end this shit tonight. You made a bad mistake tonight, old man. You should have never showed me this room. Now I'm gonna tell the cops and you're going to jail. You'll never murder anyone ever again!"

"Murder?" Henry laughed. "I have never killed anyone, or worn the bunny man costume. Because you see, Jimmy. The Bunny Man curse skips a generation."

Something moved behind Jimmy. He turned around just as he saw Heather swing her axe and hit Jimmy on his shoulder. Jimmy screamed and fell to his knees. He could feel half of his body going numb. He looked up and begged Heather not to hit him again. Heather raised her axe and this time it came down on Jimmy's head, shattering his skull and killing him instantly. Heather dropped her bloody axe and ran over to her father and hugged him.

"What will we do with his body?" Heather finally asked.

"I know a place where they will never find it. Police will come and ask questions, but eventually they will go away. They always do. I love your rabbit ears."

"Thanks, daddy."

Henry took off her bunny ears and hung them on the wall.

"There. A special place of honor. Your first killing. Your ancestors would be so proud of you."

"I love you, daddy."

Caretaker
Walt Gavenda

"Bin Laden is in the bathroom."

I looked up from the morning paper. Molly, my wife, was standing there in a bathrobe with a towel draped over one shoulder and a very nasty expression on her usually placid face.

"What?" I said. Not very original but at that particular moment I couldn't wrap my mind around the astonishing statement that Osama Bin Laden was in our bathroom.

"Which one?" I asked.

"You know. Tall. Skinny. Beard and a big nose. And a nasty temper to boot. I stuffed him into the clothes hamper." Molly's eyes were flashing little green sparks, I mean real sparks and not just metaphorical ones. I knew that look all too well and it didn't bode well for Bin Laden.

"I meant which bathroom."

"The one upstairs," she snorted. "First he asked me where Mohammed was. Then he wondered where his virgins were. Then he started yelling at me for being a shameless harlot, walking around with my hair and face uncovered." The green sparks got a little brighter.

"So then I zapped him. I left him in the clothes hamper muttering invective against all kufirs." Molly paused and looked a bit quizzical. "What's a kufir?"

"We are, Molly dear," I replied. "It means infidel, animal, a lower, ignorant life form."

"What are they thinking of in Heaven Central, sending us Bin Laden without any notice?" she asked stomping her left foot in agitation. "We've already got Hitler, and Trotsky..."

"Don't forget Attila," I said. "Attila and his damned horse in the basement. We still have to deal with him. The neighbors are complaining about the galloping sounds in the middle of the night."

I slowly got up from the chair and headed for the stairs.

"You know how screwed up the Heavenly bureaucracy is. They still haven't recovered from World War II. Take a nice bath in the downstairs bathroom. Chill a bit. I'll take care of our guest. He might just be temporary any way."

Fat chance. We were the dumping ground for all the hard cases. We were going to be stuck with Bin Laden unless he put his foot wrong and ended up in the Outer Darkness.

Molly went off towards the guest bathroom muttering to herself. Bin Laden better mind his Ps and Qs or else get used to spending a large chunk of eternity in the clothes hamper.

Bin Laden was going to be a toughie. From his actions, it didn't sound like he quite got the message. I wasn't sure how to handle him. He had to have a spark of decency somewhere, or Heaven never would have let him loose.

As I was going up the stairs mulling over the problem, Trotsky's shade was coming down.

"Good morning Leon," I said. "How's tricks?"

Trotsky looked at me with disdain. Trotsky was in a permanent state of disdain. But at least he stopped his revolutionary rants. "What was all the commotion in the bathroom? Has the revolution finally started?"

"No," I replied, "but even if it had started, it wouldn't do you any good. Get those pesky thoughts out of your mind if you ever hope to get out of here."

"Well who is in the bathroom?" snapped Trotsky.

"Osama Bin Laden."

"You mean the crazy Musselman?" said Trotsky, making a face like he swallowed castor oil.

"You better get that opium of the people crap out of your head Leon, or else you'll be stuck in your broom closet for a long, long time. You and Bin Laden will just have to get along. This may be part of your testing. Besides, you both have something in common."

"What could we possibly have in common? I am a true Bolshevik and he is a religious freako." Trotsky was waxing indignant, another thing he did very well.

"Well for starters, you both got it in the head, him with a bullet and you with an ice axe. Secondly, you're both dead guys and you are stuck here with me. Don't push me Leon."

Trotsky gulped, blanched, vaporized into an ectoplasmic mist, and slid under the door into the broom closet. Trotsky didn't like to talk about his assassination. Seemed to give him the jitters. That was one of the ways you could shut him up. I continued to trudge up the stairs wondering if it was the ghosts who were on trial, or us.

With Trotsky out of the way, for a while, I went into the bathroom, slowly opened the hamper lid and said, "Come out, come out, wherever you are."

Bin Laden popped out of the hamper like a demented jack in the box. A pair of my dirty under shorts was dangling off one ear. He still had part of his head blown away. He hadn't learned to work the ectoplasm yet.

Some spooks got really good at it. Ted Bundy (yes we got stuck with him too) could manifest as a cute little girl. He'd go out and stalk the neighborhood and scare the whey out of people. Set a swarm of ghost hunters loose on us. Heaven didn't like that. Interfered with their idea of cosmic order. He caused so many problems we had to call the Watchmen. They keep order on the ethereal plain. They're entities you don't want to mess with whether you are alive or dead.

The Watchmen whisked him off and deposited him in a convent in Cleveland run by a little known order of nuns, The Sisters of Divine Retribution. They're praying for him even now. Serves him right. I hope Bundy is learning his lesson and isn't coming back here but deep inside I doubt it.

"Who are you? Where is Mohammad? Where are my virgins?" shouted Bin Laden waving his arms around so much that he was fading into a mist.

"I'm your Caretaker." I replied. "Didn't the Welcoming Committee explain what's going to happen to you?"

"They said something about mending my soul," he huffed. He was literally bouncing off the ceiling.

"My soul doesn't need to be mended. I'm the Emir of Al Qa'ida, the sword of Allah, destined to be Caliph..."

"You're believing your own stuff, pal," I said. "Your ultimate destiny was to be gunned down in some hick town in Pakistan and you've fulfilled it. Now you've got to start over and face the rest of what's going to happen to you for what's left of eternity."

"You are lying," Bin Laden screamed. "You are a kufir, Crusader, agent of Shatain!" With that he made a lunge for me, hands outstretched, aiming for my throat.

"Pickles!" I shouted.

With a soft poof, Pickles the hellhound appeared between me and Bin Laden. Pickles weighed 250 pounds or so and was the size of a small Shetland pony. She was covered with black fur and had eyes that glowed red from within (which is never a good sign by the way.) Smoke was coming out of her ears and nostrils. And when she opened her mouth she had a set of teeth that looked like they could devour Manhattan.

Bin Laden, with a look of horror on what was left of his face jumped into the bathtub and was trying to close the shower curtain and hide behind it. He didn't have enough energy to do that so it simply rippled a little.

"Impressive," I said, smiling at Bin Laden, "isn't she?"

Bin Laden stood in the bathtub, shaking. When he finally spoke, it was rather ragged. "How can it hurt me?" he stuttered. "I'm dead."

"So is she," I replied, "and you really don't want to find out what she can do to you. It isn't very pretty."

As if to emphasize the point, Pickles snarled showing her massive teeth. Pickles and I had worked together for quite some time and had the routine down pat.

Bin Laden looked like he wanted to pass out but ghosts can't do that. He would probably succeed in falling into the coal cellar and with Attila down there who knows what would happen.

"Steady on." I said softly. "Maybe you should get back into the hamper and gather yourself together a bit."

Bin Laden looked doubtful.

"Don't worry," I said. "I'll leave the lid open. We'll talk more, later. And try to show your full face will you. It's bad enough talking to you without feeling like I'm dealing with a zombie."

Keeping a close eye (he only had one left) on Pickles he glided over to the hamper and slid on in. I gave Pickles a pat on the head.

"Good girl." I said. Pickles gave my hand a lick. It was a bit like being licked by acid dripping sand paper. Then she softly faded away.

I went back down the stairs wondering just what in the heck I would do. When I reached the bottom of the stairs a voice out of thin air said, "Incoming message from Central." Just what I needed!

"Relay the message," I said, using the standard formula.

"Expect the spiritual remains of Osama Bin Laden to arrive within the next two of your planet's days. Make all preparations to receive what may be a difficult case."

Another screw up. "He's here already you idiot!"

"What," replied Central. "How can that be?"

"You tell me, ace. Right now he's blubbering in the upstairs clothes hamper."

"I don't understand how this could happen," replied Central.

I was really getting steamed. "It happened the same way you fobbed off that ghost of an intelligent slug from Zeta Reticulae on us. Didn't even have the right damned planet. Arsenic based life form so whenever it materialized the smell would knock you over. The neighbors thought we had a meth lab. Drew all of its energy for manifesting from plants. Killed all Molly's houseplants and half the trees in the yard. The needles even fell off our Christmas tree."

"Yes," replied Central rather snottily. "Your species has the regrettable habit of killing other life forms for various fey reasons."

"The tree was artificial and then the damn thing ate all the ornaments." I was really getting hot.

"It was a simple mix-up. The creature came from the planet Yrith. Your planet is named Earth. It's easy to get these primitive names confused." Central was starting to take its, me Tarzan, you stupid tone. "Besides, the creature's spiritual remains have now gone to a place that is more compatible."

"Probably to a toxic waste dump somewhere," I muttered. "So what am I supposed to do with the shade of a crazed Arab mass murderer?"

"Handle it," said the voice. "You're good at these difficult cases anyway."

With that there was pop, and it was gone.

"You can't leave it like this," I screamed. "Come back you miserable…"

I felt the warm touch of Molly's arm around my waste. "Calm yourself. There's nothing we can do. They will never admit a mistake. We'll just have to handle it."

So we did. Pickles, Molly and I managed to coax Bin Laden out of the hamper. He had to leave so we could get our dirty clothes out. He didn't want to leave at first so we threatened to send him through the rinse cycle in the washer. We took the hamper up to the spare bedroom closet and put Bin Laden back into it, which was something else again. We told him to stay there until he could act in a reasonable way or the universe ended, whichever came first.

The spare room was a good choice. We never had any visitors, at least live ones. Those rare visitors who had to come to the house for some reason, usually kept their stay short and no one ever wanted to spend the night. Can't say that I blame them.

Before I go on, I've got a little explaining to do so you can understand what's going on here. Every living soul gets one last chance when it dies, even Hitler, Trotsky and Bin Laden. You get a choice. You can try to fix your miserable shriveled soul, or you can go to the Outer Darkness. I've seen and heard the Outer Darkness as part of my Caretaker training, and that's a pale description of what it's really like. Osama must have asked for and been granted a final chance, whether he realizes it or not.

Now just because you say you're sorry and all that, it doesn't mean you get an immediate ticket to the Choir Invisible. You have to linger on earth, changing your ways, getting rid of your evil ideas and habits. But some people are such that they need to be watched. So Caretakers, in this case Molly and me, are assigned to keep them out of trouble. And most of these clowns are trouble magnets.

We couldn't have Bin Laden's ghost popping up at the State Department or Ground Zero, nor could we have Hitler popping up at the UN. It's bad enough with the live loonies that show up there.

22

Now Molly and I weren't around when Attila the Hun ravaged Europe. We inherited him and Trotsky and Hitler from the previous Caretakers. No wonder they looked so happy to move on. We'll probably be passing them plus Bin Laden off to whatever sucker…ah…kindly couple, takes our place. And I hope it's soon.

Things went along smoothly, well smooth for us, chaos for any normal person, for the next week or so. Trotsky stayed in his closet. I think he was beginning to like it in there. Hitler remained in the attic dormer, playing my old Beatles collection over and over. Who'd have thought that one of the worst mass murderers of the twentieth century would end up digging 60s rock. Or maybe he was trying to torture us by playing "Yellow Submarine" over and over again. I wouldn't put it past him. I'm not sure what Attila was doing, but at least he was quiet.

Not so with Bin Laden. He kept trying to sneak out of the hamper and leave the house, which was impossible because he was attached to the house unlike Ted Bundy, who for some reason, was not. Another screw up. Bin Laden needed a material anchor to manifest and the house was it. He couldn't leave until we moved him or he met heavenly standards, which for him was a chancy proposition at best.

It was a Sunday afternoon in October. I'd just thrown Bin Laden out of the flour bin and back to his hamper and told Pickles to watch him. He didn't like Molly, who besides being a woman took no guff.

"I can't deal with that woman with the green sparks," he whined as I chivied him out of the flour bin.

"You mean sparks like this?" I replied as little blue sparks flew out of my eyes. It was one of the tricks we learned at the Caretakers Academy. I got an A in eye sparks. Got a D in diplomacy.

Bin Laden zoomed up the stairs to the spare room with Pickles on his tail. Things were quiet again. Today the Redskins were playing the Cowboys. I was going to relax and watch some football. Like hell.

When I got to the living room, Hitler was on television, giving a speech, in English. Hitler loved television but fortunately the only television he could get on, was mine.

23

"Adolph," I shouted. "What did I tell you about Sunday afternoons?"

Hitler stopped and tried to smile in his most ingratiating way. Made him look like a constipated baboon. "Please sir," he said. "I've been working on this speech for a long time and I need to practice."

"Sunday afternoon is football!"

"*Ach du lieber*," he replied with a theatrical shake of his head. "Football, football. Is that all you think about? A good German team could wipe the field with the *untermench* you got playing now."

"Just like your army wiped the field with our army in World War II eh?"

Not the right thing to say just at that moment, but I was a bit upset. I'd have a time getting him off the TV.

Suddenly the doorbell rang. What now? Nobody ever comes here.

I opened the door and my heart jumped into my mouth. It was Frank, our nosy neighbor who was a ghost hunter to boot. He must have been a sensitive because he knew something was weird about the house and had been trying for years to get me to allow his group in for a ghost hunt.

I turned him down every time. That's all I'd need is to have some medium on his team channeling Hitler or Trotsky. And the boyos would relish their chance to go through their spook tricks. We'd have every ghost show on cable beating a path to our door. We'd be featured in the weird press. And Heaven Central would be very, very upset.

"What can I do for you Frank?" I said, trying to block his way in. He slipped by me anyway. I could see that he had a K-2 meter, which measures electro-magnetic radiation, fastened to his belt and it was going nuts.

He stopped at the living room door. "Isn't that Hitler on television?"

"Yes," I replied, trying to hustle him along towards the kitchen. But he wouldn't budge.

"But he's speaking English," Frank said glancing down at the K-2.

"Most people don't know that Hitler was a great linguist. This is a History Channel special. *The Hidden Life of Hitler*." It was the best I could do at the moment.

I had to get Hitler off the tube because I knew Frank wasn't going to buy it. I shot a thought to Pickles. "Pickles, Hitler, television, now."

Hitler continued to speak even faster. Suddenly there was a growl behind him, the screen went a little crazy and in place of Hitler a football game appeared, a game from 1955 in black and white. The faint odor of sulfur filled the air.

Frank was looking a little queasy and the K-2 was still going nuts. "I thought I saw a big black dog with glowing eyes on the screen."

"Well I've been having trouble with the DVR. Short or something like that. That probably was that Harry Potter movie with the big dog in it. Molly loves Harry Potter." I was treading water and sinking fast.

"I remember this game from when I was a kid," Frank said his eyes growing even wider. "This looks like the original broadcast. There's Otto Graham and little Eddie La Baron."

"It's an NFL channel classic. They have them every Sunday before the regular games." Crap! Hitler screwed up the time stream again. I hope the TV was the only thing that was being affected. If Frank walked out the door into 1955, I could never explain it.

Suddenly there was a thumping and bumping coming from upstairs. Much to my dismay, Pickles, in corporeal form was plunging down the stairs followed by Molly. Frank took one look and passed out cold. So much for the intrepid ghost hunter.

Molly was standing there catching her breath. Pickles was sniffing at Frank.

"What happened?" I asked.

"We had to do something or else," she replied.

"What do we do now?" I said. My mind was too muddled to think clearly and who knew when Frank would wake up.

"First we'll put him in the recliner," Molly said. It's a darn good thing Frank was a little guy or we would never have made it.

"Now what?"

"Get him a beer, fill the glass half full, and put it on the table next to him. Oh good, the regular football game has come on."

I went out to the kitchen as instructed, filled half the glass and then put it on the TV table next to Frank who was beginning to stir.

"Follow my lead," whispered Molly as we both sat on the couch.

Frank shook his head, blinked several times and bolted straight up. "Where's the dog?" he gasped. Pickles had long since vanished.

"We don't have a dog Frank. We're both allergic," Molly said sweetly.

"But I saw a huge black dog with red glowing eyes," he shouted. "And Hitler was on television shouting in English and then the '55 Redskins came on!"

"Frank," I said, "you came in, sat down in the recliner, I gave you a beer, we talked a bit about your family and then you nodded off. You looked so peaceful I didn't want to wake you."

"But I saw the dog, I saw Hitler yelling in English, then I saw…"

"Frank, you must have had a lulu of a dream," I said. "First of all, Hitler never spoke English. Secondly, you can see that it's today's burgundy and gold on the field." The band was playing "Hail to the Redskins."

Frank ripped the K-2 from the pouch on his belt. It looked dead. "See," he shouted, " that monster dog must have drained the battery in the K-2."

"Are you sure it's on?" said Molly.

Frank fumbled with the switch on the side. All the lights on the K-2 lit up and settled at the lowest reading. He looked up sheepishly. "I don't know what to say."

He shakily got out of the chair, took a quick glance up the stairs and headed for the door. "I think I'd better go," he said.

"Do you have to leave so soon? Finish your brew and watch some of the game with me."

"Yes," Molly said. "I was just was saying the other day that we don't see enough of you."

"Yeah," said Frank, still looking bewildered. "Uhh, thanks for the beer, I guess." He rushed out the door and ran down the front walk, looking back over his shoulder.

"Whew!" Molly and I said in unison.

"Close call, eh sweets?" I said. "Thank the Almighty you're clever."

Molly just smiled, that knowing smile that women sometimes have when they know something you don't.

Things calmed down a bit after that. Hitler apologized profusely but then he always does and then does something crazy again. He dropped the 60s and is now playing non-stop Scott Joplin ragtime. Trotsky stayed in the closet muttering things about the dictatorship of the proletariat. I don't think he's ever going to get out of here.

Bin Laden still hasn't come to terms with things. I've given him the lecture and video about the Outer Darkness and that seemed to calm him down for a bit. I told him he'd have to improve a lot more if he wanted to get out of the clothes hamper. Attila is still quiet, but something big is coming from him. No mystery why he's been down here so long. Pickles has cleaned all the rats out of the neighborhood. And when I see Frank on the street, he quickly walks the other way. Can't really blame him.

Farewell Washington
Randall N. Dunn

"The last enemy that shall be destroyed is death."
I Corinthians 15:26

Bradley Whitcomb studied his daughter, Anne, with concern. She sat across from him at the large oval cherry conference table; the 22 year-old brunette's shoulders shaking, tears dripping onto an open magazine. He noticed she hadn't turned the page in at least 30 minutes.

He stood, came around the table, knelt and held her hands. "What can I do, Popsicle?"

"I miss Mom something awful." She wiped her face with the sleeve of her Penn State sweatshirt. "Why did it have to happen? Why did she have to die? We didn't even get to give her a burial."

"I know. I miss her too. It's like my life has been torn from me."

"It has, Daddy." She looked up, studying her father's sad, bloodshot eyes. "Mom was your soul mate."

Bradley Whitcomb held his daughter's gaze a moment. "It's a tragedy, that's for sure."

"But why did it have to happen? Who would do something so awful? I mean, the entire world is gone."

"Well, we're holding out for pockets of hope. That's what Captain Riley is trying to determine now." Whitcomb glanced over to Air Force Captain Kathy Riley, who operated the communication station in the President's Emergency Operations Center (PEOC), twelve stories under the White House.

Riley shot him a grim look, shaking her head.

He returned his attention to his daughter. "We'll be safe down here, Popsicle."

"But for how long? And we've lost Mom."

"I know." He brushed tears from her cheeks with his thumbs. "I'm so very sorry about Mom. Tragically unfair. But she would want us to go on. You know that, don't you? We mustn't give up. For Mom's sake. All right?"

"Mmm—How long, Daddy?"

"With just the three of us? We can live down here for a couple of years. Maybe more if we can figure out how to start the hydroponic gardens."

"But what about power? Someone has to man and feed the power generators topside and there's no one left."

"Can you keep a secret?"

She grimaced. "Who could I possibly leak it to? *The Washington Post*? Bill O'Reilly."

"Good point." He chucked her under her chin. "We have a small nuclear generator below us. We'll have power for a hundred years."

She threw her hands in the air. "That's just great! Live in this bunker for a hundred years? I don't think so."

"No, sweetheart. I have something else in mind. Your Dad's not going to let you down again." He cupped her cheek and kissed her on the forehead. "I'll be right back. I need to look into that plan I promised you." He forced a thin smile. "We'll be okay. We'll get through this together."

He stood and stepped over to Captain Riley, placing a fatherly hand on her shoulder. "How's it going, Kathy?"

"Not well, Mr. President. I'm currently in comms with senior leadership of the British government. In addition to five souls in the command bunker in London, they estimate maybe two dozen survivors nationwide."

"The Prime Minister?"

"Sorry, Sir." She shook her head. "I know he was a friend of yours."

"How about the Russians?" The President stuffed his hands in his trouser pockets.

"I'm afraid not, sir. Lost comms with them an hour ago. I fear they're gone. The Russian Defense Minister said they were all infected. His last words were an apology to the world. Uh— what's left of it, that is. The bug was something they had created. It was stolen over a year ago and they didn't report it."

"Damn Russians. Anything else?"

"Yes sir. Interestingly, the Defense Minister's last action was to transmit all engineering files on the bug in hopes that we can design a vaccine."

"A little late for that, isn't it?"

"Um, yeah. But not for the few survivors." She studied the President. "Sir, we must find a way to continue the human race. We can't give up."

The President sighed. "Yes, Kathy. I understand. What else do you have?"

"The funny thing is, Sir, the creator of that bug or whatever that hell on earth is–well–um–he–he's onboard the International Space Station. He's the ISS Chief Scientist."

"Good Lord."

"Yeah, pretty odd coincidence, isn't it?" She rushed on. "So I was thinking, Sir. You see–the Defense Minister's email did say that if all else fails, the bug goes inert in 25 years. And seeing that this heinous creation's creator is onboard the ISS, I took the liberty of uploading all files to the space station's science team." She looked panged. "It's just—just—"

"Just in case we don't make it?" The President held Kathy's eyes. "We will. I've let so many down these past few weeks. I won't let you down."

"Thank you, Sir. I believe in you. And you've not let anyone down, Sir."

Whitcomb knitted his brow. "Anything else?"

"I'm in contact with a few survivors in the alternate command bunker at Offutt Air Force Base, and about a dozen or so in Cheyenne Mountain."

"What about the Antarctic? Surely they couldn't have been infected."

"Lost McMurdo Station thirty minutes ago. Last comms with them was a goodbye. They said they were infected by someone off the last C-160 re-supply mission." She tilted her head, studying her gloss-black dress shoes. "I'm sorry, Mr. President. I should have kept you in the loop."

"It's okay, Kathy. It's not as if I could do anything about it." He lifted her chin with his fingers until their eyes met. "That being said, we should be on a first name basis. Don't you think?"

"Um, yes, Mr. President. I mean—I don't think I can do this."

"Try it. You'll get used to it." He patted her shoulder. "By the way, have you been in voice contact with the ISS?"

"Yes, Sir. I mean—"

He smiled; something he hadn't done in the past several weeks since the world-wide epidemic broke out, a monstrous disease from which his wife was one of the first casualties in Washington D.C.. "Go on, Kathy."

She gripped the console. "Yes, Bradley. We're in constant comms. The crew members are in good physical health with no contamination from the latest re-supply tug. They miss their families though, and the two docs are pretty busy treating several cases of depression. And they had a suicide last night."

"Good Lord. What happened?"

"One of the engineers couldn't bear the loss of his wife and three children. He stepped into an airlock and out into space."

"Without a pressure suit, I presume."

"Uh-huh."

"Ugh." The President hung his head. "Any good news?"

"Yes. The ISS has enough food stores and supplies for several years. In addition, they have several years of food, water, fuel, and O_2 generation units in low earth orbit storage tugs. And their new hydroponic gardens are producing more food every day. In addition to the 40 onboard crew, they'll be able to house and feed up to a hundred additional people for several years. And that's without building additional housing modules, for which they have supplies on the deep orbit warehouse. They're prepared to begin construction immediately."

"I'm not certain we'll find a hundred people alive on this entire planet," the President said. "But this is good news. Which brings me to my next question. Is the space station in contact with the Mars Mission?"

"Yes. And the MMV III is on a high speed trajectory away from Mars, returning to Earth orbit."

"Good. Very good. Do you think it'll work, Kathy?"

"It's a solid plan, Sir. I think it can."

"So do I. Let me know if anything develops." He held Kathy by the shoulders. "I'm sorry about your losses."

Her eyes were moist and rimmed red. "Thank you. That means so very much to me."

He studied her, thinking back over the years to when she

was a little girl. He had served in the Air Force with her father. They had lived on the same cul-de-sac for years. His oldest daughter, Amanda, and Kathy had been best friends. Until that tragic winter afternoon, when Amanda fell through the ice while skating. Kathy had tried to save her, nearly losing her own life.

And now the thought of Kathy losing her entire family in this catastrophe broke his heart. He reached out and held her hand. "Kathy. I want you to know that I now consider you my other daughter. From this point on we're family. You got that?"

She broke down and buried her head in the President's chest. After a minute, she whispered, "Thank you."

The third Mars Mission Vehicle—or MMV III—was the largest space vehicle man had ever built. As large as a Navy guided missile cruiser—its tear drop shape gives it a sleekness unmatched in the history of space travel. It has three levels, six massive ion-drive engines, a crew of ten, berthing for fifty passengers and numerous large cargo bays.

On board, were two surface exploration vehicles, called SEVs, with the capacity for three crew, twelve passengers and a modest cargo bay. They were built to shuttle between the MMV III and the Mars surface. But in a few short hours, they will be used for an earth orbital insertion.

The MMV III had been working on continuing the five year-long construction of the growing Mars colony for the past six months and wasn't due to rotate back to earth orbit for another year. But the ship's commander and crew now found themselves on the most extraordinary mission of their careers: to save Earth's survivors.

The first transmission the commander received four weeks ago was simply:

"MAYDAY—MAYDAY— MAYDAY—ELE!"

ELE?

Commander Stanton had to look that one up.

When the MMV's onboard computer spit out the answer, he sucked in his breath. The Earth had experienced an Extinction Life Event—something only imaginable in SciFi movies. But to his horror, this ELE was not fiction. And now he and his crew found themselves the sole lifeline to any remaining inhabitants of Earth. And it was to begin, and possibly end, in Washington D.C.

Stanton spoke into his comms headset, "Jenn?"

"Yes, Commander?"

"Please calculate the burn time for orbital insert. We have a date to keep. And please display results on screen three."

"Roger, Commander. Coming up."

Stanton studied the plasma displays on his instrument console, then called, "Engineering?"

"Yes, Skipper. Drake here."

"Main engine status please."

"Skipper, all Ion-drives are nominal and fully charged."

"Thanks, Drake." Stanton checked display three, tapped in a few calculations on his computer: then called, "Jenn?"

"Yes, Commander."

"Prepare for roll sequencing and Max-V burn. I agree with your calculations. We'll begin orbit insert on your mark."

"Copy that. Vehicle roll and Max-V burn in three. Orbit insert on my mark."

Stanton studied the display, tapping his keyboard. "Jenn, all looks a go. You may initiate auto roll sequencer 4A5 on program timer mode. Begin Max-V insertion burn at your discretion."

"Roger that. Orbit insert geometry plotted and laid in. Auto roll 4A5 and Max-V burn on my mark."

Stanton punched a button on his comms console. "Computer, display orbital graphics on screen one." He next swiveled in his flight chair, facing his First Officer. "Close her down, Alex. We're going home. Or to whatever's left of it."

"Roger that, Skipper. Ship's as tight as a muskrat's sphincter."

President Whitcomb had asked both Anne and Kathy if they'd like a sandwich but they declined. He made himself a baloney, cheese, and mustard sandwich on white bread. He knew he should eat healthy wheat, but he reasoned since the world had gone to hell in a hand basket, who cared about wheat bread? Besides, it's plain blasphemy to have a baloney sandwich on anything other than white bread.

He grabbed a bottle of water from the refrigerator and settled into an overstuffed burgundy leather chair in the conference room's alcove to contemplate their future. After a few minutes he glanced at the blank flat screen TV recessed into the wall. It hadn't been turned on in a week. No need to power it up. There weren't any more TV transmissions.

He took a bite of his sandwich while recalling the press reports in the first days after the world-wide epidemic. Apparently, an international religious cult had decided to end all life on Earth by spreading a genetically engineered plague across every continent on the planet. They had planned the attack for years and had operatives in place in all major cities and at all major transportation nodes—air, rail, truck, ship—prepared to release the plague when the signal was given. And on the fateful day, the cult leader interrupted all world-wide broadcasts— terrestrial and satellite radio, TV and Internet—with the following message:

"The Lord saw how great man's wickedness on the Earth had become, and that every inclination of the thoughts of his heart was only evil all the time. The Lord was grieved that he had made man on the Earth, and his heart was filled with pain. So the Lord said, "I will wipe mankind, whom I have created, from the face of the Earth."

"God has spoken to us. And the Lord thy God has told us His patience with mankind's continuous life of vile sin has run out. In His infinite wisdom, the Lord Almighty has declared a second end to humankind. He has, therefore, chosen us as His emissaries to end all human life on this planet. When this is complete, He will begin again with sinless man, just as he had planned with the first Adam and Eve. So say goodbye wicked inhabitants of this fallen world, for God has chosen to smite thee all."

President Whitcomb rubbed his face with his hands, remembering that no one—not all the religious leaders of the

34

world, not the United Nations nor the major intelligence services believed this raving lunatic. They had surmised it impossible for a nation state, let alone a single cult personality, to have the wherewithal to destroy all life on earth. But they were wrong.

Tragically wrong.

In three days, masses around the world began falling ill and dying. And two months later, nearly every inhabitant on Earth had succumbed to the plague.

Whitcomb set down his half-eaten sandwich, thinking of his wife. An advocate of early childhood reading, she had been leading a group of grade school children on a tour of the Library of Congress—ground zero for the D.C. attack.

He'd been in the PEOC bunker at the time it happened. He and Captain Riley had been giving his daughter a tour of one of the most sophisticated communication systems in the world. Anne had recently graduated from the Pennsylvania State University with a major in communication engineering and was thinking of joining the Air Force like her father and Kathy.

After about an hour, the two Secret Service agents with them had gone topside to retrieve a working lunch for the three. Five minutes later, alarms went off and the vault door to the PEOC automatically sealed, leaving the three of them stranded below ground.

Safe below ground.

Alone, 120 feet below ground.

Now, among only a few dozen to a hundred survivors of the earth's first ELE, the President shook his head. *An Extinction Life Event. Good Lord in Heaven.*

He glanced at the blank TV screen again, remembering the last hours. News reporters had been filming around the clock in front of the Capital Building, the White House, even at the base of the Washington Monument and along the reflecting pool.

The city was all but deserted as the reporters warned people to stay off the streets. "Stay home and spend your last days with loved ones," they repeated. Then, the news teams fell too ill to continue their reporting, and made their way to their homes and families to wait for the veil of death to descend.

President Whitcomb buried his head in his hands, visualizing his wife's emaciated corpse alone in her "death chair" twelve stories above him. He last spoke with her by phone twelve days ago. The plague had taken her swiftly. For that, he was thankful. Most had suffered long agonizing deaths. But for Cheryl, there wasn't a thing the finest doctors in the world could do. With no antidote, they were dying almost as quickly as she.

His last moments with her over the phone were filled with her describing the beauty of Washington D.C. in the spring. She sat in her chair in front of their large picture window overlooking the Ellipse and the Washington Monument. She described the pink flowering cherry trees, the colorful gardens rimming the White House, and ancient green oaks strewn throughout the city parks.

But the thousands of tourists from across the globe, who normally filled the city with such vibrant life and energy, were mostly absent. There were a few, his wife said, who aimlessly wandered the streets and parks. They either didn't receive word that the end was upon them, or they had nowhere to go and die. So they would perish on the streets of the greatest city on Earth.

They talked this way for some time. Then she said in a whisper, "Goodbye, my love."

It was over.

His Cheryl was gone and he would never hold or kiss her again. At least she had passed watching the city she loved.

The city of her birth. The city of her death.

All he could do now was close his eyes and try to imagine them walking hand-in-hand through the White House flower gardens she cherished.

After several minutes he stood, shook the thoughts from his head, and made his way to his daughter; convinced in his soul that his most important duty from here on was not to the United States or democracy in the free world. It was to comfort and protect Anne and Kathy.

Commander Stanton radioed the crew. "All right. Good orbital insert, team." He checked the data readouts on the computer displays before him, tapped a few keys, then radioed his communications officer. "Comms."

"Yes, Skipper."

"Have you been in contact with the Space Station?"

"Roger that. ISS is standing by to assist. And they're ready to receive the President and his party."

"Very good. Tell them we'll begin deorbit burns within the hour."

He switched his mental focus, taking in the large blue and white globe rotating below him. Perfect from this distance—pristine and beautiful. But he knew better now.

As the MMV passed over North America, Stanton made out the East Coast, the eclipse of night approaching. Somewhere down there, he thought, is Washington D.C. And somewhere in that city are the President and his daughter miraculously alive. And Captain Riley. Odd thought amidst such calamity. But he was very much looking forward to seeing Kathy again.

"Nav," he radioed. "How long can we sustain this orbit?"

"How long do you need, Skipper?"

"Long enough to map the earth for live inhabitants."

"No problem, Skipper."

"All right then. I'd like for you and the First Officer to remain behind and commence scanning while I lead the advance team to the surface to recover the President and his party. And hopefully, after the President, we'll need to make several more landings."

"Roger that."

Stanton turned his attention back to his flight console, studying a mirage of digital readouts. "All right, crew. Let's get both SEVs prepped for de-orbit. We don't want to keep the President waiting. I'll fly *Deliverance,* to pick up the President and party, and I want *Patience* to provide cover and backup."

The SEVs, *Deliverance* and *Patience,* were named after their ancient sailing counterparts: the two original wooden-hulled ships that were built from the wreckage of their mothership, the doomed *Sea Venture.* In 1609, she sailed from England to America. While on her way to save the failing settlement at Jamestown, Virginia, the *Sea Venture* ran aground in a storm on the uncharted reefs of Bermuda. A year later, with the building of the *Deliverance* and *Patience* complete, the two small crews set sail to assist the ravaged and struggling colony at Jamestown. But the thirty-two ton *Patience* vanished; believed to this day to have been lost in the Bermuda Triangle.

Stanton's commset crackled, bringing him back to the present. "Skipper, Nav here."

"Go, Nav."

"I've located the President and his party. I've also commenced scanning for other life, but a large magnetic storm has moved in, making it near impossible. That storm's also degrading our comms with the PEOC."

"Copy that, Nav. We'll go in blind if we have to. Have you transmitted our intentions?"

"Yes, sir. They know you'll be arriving soon."

"Good copy. Stay on it."

"Roger that. Nav out."

Anne watched her father staring at the blank TV screen. She knew he was grieving, thinking of his wife of nearly thirty years—of her mother. She wanted to comfort him, but she was empty—her soul drained. She moved to him and gave him a long silent hug. Then she kissed him on the cheek, and stepped across the large conference room to Kathy in the comm room, who was just finishing a conversation with someone.

"Hi, Kathy. Who you talking with?"

"The MMV. They're preparing to send an orbital lander for us."

"We're being evacuated? To space?"

"Yeah. That's good news."

"I guess. But I don't want to leave Mom. I don't want to leave Washington."

Kathy turned and held Anne's hands. "Listen, honey, it'll be all right. First of all, your Mom has already left. She's in a far better place than us. And I know she would want you to move on. To move forward and be a part of something larger than yourself. Maybe even rebuild this world." She forced a smile. "You understand, Anne?"

"Yeah, I think so. If we want to save this world—this city—we'll need to save ourselves first."

"There you go."

"So what's next?"

"Well, in a couple of hours there'll be a knock on the blast door. We'll be in our bio-hazard suits and—"

"Our what?"

"Bio-hazard suits. We can't go out there exposed to that virus, or plague, or whatever that hideous hell on Earth is."

"Where'd we get bio-hazard suits?"

"Honey, we're talking about the President and his daughter here. This bunker is equipped with everything need for survival in almost any disaster. Man-made or natural."

"Well, isn't that just peachy. So we dress up in these Bozo suits and trundle off with a bunch of astronauts. To where?"

"The current plan is first to the International Space Station. And perhaps Mars after that."

"Mars! Freakin' *Mars?* What are we gonna do on *Mars?*"

"We'll live there, I guess. And reproduce, I suppose. Until it's safe to return to Earth with a new generation of star children."

"Yeah. Whatever."

"Seriously, Anne. Given the dire circumstances, your dad has a pretty good plan.

Anne shrugged. "Okay, so how can I help? You want me to get the Bozo suits ready?"

"Sure. That's a great idea. They're in the equipment room. You can't miss them. Big, orange, and dopey looking. If you can drag three out for us, we'll be ready to go when we hear that knock on the door."

They descended from the MMV as a pair, in loose formation. Two cobalt-gray landing vehicles shaped much like their mother ship, but a fraction of the size. Unlike the MMV, her SEVs were designed for both orbital and sub-orbital flight with retractable vertical stabilizers and wings.

On the other hand, like their mother ship, they also used ion drives for flight, but only two each were needed, and they were much smaller units. One drive each mounted on the port and starboard pressure hulls. The ion-drives operated on computer controlled gimbals, allowing the pilot complete maneuverability, to include landing the vehicle in a horizontal position on its retractable landing gear. For lateral yaw and vertical pitch while maneuvering in space, each SEV had several reaction control thrusters mounted forward and aft.

"All right, team," Commander Stanton called into his comms set, "We've successfully deorbited and the computer has us on a direct approach to D.C. I'll bring *Deliverance* down on the White House front lawn. *Patience,* I'd like you to remain airborne, providing combat air patrol in case we have any unforeseen visitors. And don't bug out on me, getting lost in the Bermuda Triangle. I want to see you on my wing on return to orbit. You got that?"

"Copy that, Skipper," Jenn radioed, flying *Patience* in formation a hundred yards off Deliverance's starboard wing. "I'll provide CAP. We've got all sensors humming. No sign of life yet. Altitude 78,000 feet. Weather on the ground should be favorable for a visual approach, but we've got heavy cloud cover extending from 31,000 feet down to 3,000. Also a raging T-Storm system in the area that's going to be dicey maneuvering around. How copy?"

"Ah, that's a good copy. Not much chance of running into any airliners. We'll let the computers fly us through the cloud deck and around the storm, then a manual approach."

"Copy that, Skipper. I've got the White House plotted and laid in. Just waiting for a visual."

"Dad!" Anne called. "I think they're here!" She trudged toward the elevator, her bulky bio-suit halfway on.

"That's affirmative," Kathy called after her. "They just radioed. They're outside the blast door now."

The President made his way over to Kathy at the comms console, lowering his voice. "Did they give an assessment?"

"Like a ghost town. They said not a living human in sight. But there are birds and squirrels. Even two Park Police horses loitering in Lafayette Park, munching on grass."

"This city sure has taken a turn for the macabre," the

President said. "At least it looks like the animals will survive."
He laid a hand on her shoulder. "All right then, Kathy. We better
be on our way. Let's suit up and power this place down before
Anne leaves us in the dust. Tell topside we'll be ready in fifteen
minutes."

"Will do."

Commander Stanton shook the President's hand.
"Welcome aboard the *Deliverance,* Mr. President."

"Thank you, Commander. We greatly appreciate your
service." Whitcomb glanced around the cabin. *"Deliverance*, you
say?" He arched an eyebrow. "Bermuda. Jamestown. Salvation?"

"The very one, sir. Well, the 21st century version."
Stanton patted the ship's inner pressure hull. "A lot faster and
much safer."

The President pumped Stanton's hand. "Thank you, son.
We appreciate the rescue."

"My pleasure, Sir. And if you don't mind, Mr. President,
instead of Jamestown, Virginia, my crew and I would like to
shuttle you and your party up to the Space Station, then both my
SEVs will begin return missions to earth in order to rescue any
other survivors."

"Very well, Commander. Sounds like a good plan."

Stanton turned to Anne. "And Ms. Whitcomb, I am very
sorry for your loss. If there is anything my crew or myself can do
to make you comfortable please don't hesitate to ask." He shook
her hand.

"Thank you, Commander." She forced a thin smile.
"You've gone far out of your way to rescue us. I can't think of
anything else at the moment."

Stanton nodded then turned his attention to Captain Riley.
"It's good to see you again, Kathy. Unfortunate circumstances,
but it's a pleasure nonetheless."

"You too, Major."

"Once we're in orbit, please feel free to make your way to
the flight deck. I'll give you a personal tour." He smiled and
excused himself.

Anne turned to Kathy and whispered, "He's way cute.

41

You know him?"

"Yeah. We served a tour together at NASA a few years ago."

"Did you ever date?"

"No. All business."

"Hmm. A shame."

"It's not too late." She winked.

Before ascending into orbit, the President requested Commander Stanton to maneuver the *Deliverance* down Constitution Avenue. He wanted to say goodbye to his city—the greatest city on earth.

They came to a hover in front of the majestic Lincoln Memorial with *Patience* orbiting a thousand feet above. President Whitcomb admired the memorial a moment, then saluted his hero. "Take care of this city, Mr. President. Until we return."

Next, the *Deliverance* glided east, past the reflection pool and the Washington Monument, and down the Washington Mall, passing the noble Smithsonian Museum buildings on either side.

The President pointed out the oval port-hole. "It's sad to think this magnificent city will go unkempt for 25 or 30 years," he said to Anne. He scanned the blocks and blocks of streets devoid of living people. "But it's not nearly as beautiful without her residents, her tourists. The ubiquitous taxis, busses, bikers and runners. Pick-up soccer games in the parks. The sweet fragrance of flowers. The smell of international food wafting out of her magnificent restaurants. This city was so alive then."

The *Deliverance* soon came to a hover in front of the Capital Building, and Whitcomb studied it in silence until Anne squeezed his hand.

"What is it, Daddy?"

"This city's architecture is marvelous. Nothing quite like it on this planet. Come to think of it, all this granite and marble will never go to ruin." He turned to her. "We'll return, Popsicle. We definitely will. And this city will be waiting for us; and for the next generation astronauts."

As *Deliverance* ascended into orbit, The President, Anne, and Kathy sat in the smaller of two passenger compartments amidships, buckled into form-fitting flight chairs, unable to peel their eyes from the high-definition image of the retreating earth on the large flat screen display in front of them. The stunning images reminded Anne of an episode from 'The Blue Planet.'

"Look at the lights, Daddy." Anne pointed. "You can make out every landmark in the city." She pointed again. "Look! The Capital building. And over there, our home. That's where Mom—" She hung her head and went silent.

Bradley Whitcomb stroked his daughter's hair. "Yes, it's beautiful," he said sighing. "The lights will soon wink out. But rest assured, Popsicle. In time, we will return and we'll bring that great city back to life. With an entire new generation to inhabit it, walk its streets, visit its great museums. And one day, a new First Family will move into the White House."

After several minutes, Anne felt the weightlessness of space in her stomach, her body gently straining upward against her seat harness. She turned to her father. "Daddy, I was thinking one good thing could come out of this tragedy."

"Yeah? I'd like to hear some good news."

She smiled, arching her eyebrows. "I bet between this spaceship, the space station, and the Mars colony, there'll be plenty of handsome and available astronauts."

"More than enough for the two of us, as well as any female astronauts." Kathy winked.

"And tell me," the President said, playing along. "After you two get married, I suppose you want to have the first star babies."

"Yes," both women said in unison.

"And what will you name the little guys?"

"Girl, Daddy. A girl. And I'll name her, Eve."

"A boy," Kathy said. "I'd like to have a boy. And, well then…I'll just have to name him Adam."

"That sounds wonderful, ladies. I fully support your decision."

"And they'll be the first astronauts born in space," Anne said.

"And they'll be the first of their generation back to Earth,"

Kathy added.

The President grinned. "And maybe one will be our first space-born president." He took a hand each of Anne and Kathy into his and squeezed.

"Until then, ladies, let us bid farewell to Washington."

History Lesson

M.B. Wallace

   An orange-white-purple cloud ballooned upward, a deadly mushroom on a towering stalk in the sky. Houses and businesses were swept away to disappear like dry leaves in a winter gale. Shrieks filled the air; they were lost, unheard, in the roar of the shockwave that followed. Burning faces frozen in hopeless screams appeared everywhere, even reflected in the shining silver skin of the aircraft in front of her, or at least that's what Jen envisioned.

   She shook her head and stepped away from the railing, wondering why her boss had decided to hold the November financial status meeting at the Smithsonian Air and Space Museum's Udvar-Hazy Center near Dulles Airport. Everyone else in Jen's department had been enthusiastic at the chance to see the museum, but to Jen this collection was a dusty parking lot of fossils appealing only to engineers and ancient men who told the same threadbare war stories over and over, a place loaded with boring obsolete machines and the abomination that stood in front of her: the Enola Gay.

   Jen remembered the plane's name from an article in the *Washington Post*, an article that documented the outrage some of the public had felt at the Smithsonian's decision to exhibit the aircraft at its newest museum. Most people considered the Boeing B-29 Superfortress that had dropped the first atomic bomb on the city of Hiroshima too controversial to display, the paper had said. Jen used a deep sigh to sweep the remaining images of destruction and victims from her mind.

   "Beautiful old gal, isn't she?"

   Jen spun. Beside her stood a white-haired, ancient man. Jen said nothing, certain her expression voiced her disagreement. Please don't tell a war story, she silently begged.

   "She was state of the art in her time, young lady." He pointed to several areas of the craft. "Pressurized compartments, improved Wright engines, advanced radar, and that new-model

Norden bombsight. You could drop a bomb in a pickle barrel with it."

"They killed so many people, though." Jen met his eyes. "This plane dropped a nuke, for God's sake. I've seen pictures. People with huge running blisters on their faces, people with their clothes burned into their skin, or even worse."

The old man took a step toward her. "Ever heard of Pearl Harbor, hon? Guadalcanal? The Bataan Death March? How about what they did to the Chinese? The Japs weren't the friendliest people back then."

"Everyone's heard of Pearl Harbor, but—"

"Over there's a plane with a swastika on it. Nazi sons of bitches killed six million people, but I don't see you over there frowning at that one."

Jen took a drawn out breath and forced her voice to stay even. "That's true. But this plane carried a nuclear bomb. The first one. It killed all those people instantly—thousands of them—and then probably thousands more died from radiation. And it destroyed the entire city. Then the whole arms race thing started."

"Emperor Hirohito was nuts—had his whole country believing he was a god. Did you know they would have fought to the last man, woman, and child? They had orders to do that, and they were ready to do it. They would have wiped themselves out. They were holding back their best planes and pilots, waiting for us. Women and kids were supposed to grab these long bamboo spears and fight. We all would have been wading hip-deep in blood if we'd invaded the way some people still say we should have. Crazy." He gazed at nothing for a moment, his eyes unfocused, as though grasping at some elusive memory. "This old gal probably saved your grandpa's life." He squinted at Jen. "Well, maybe your great-grandpa's."

A picture of her great-grandfather's wrinkled face slipped into Jen's mind. He'd been in the Navy long ago, and from time to time had mentioned something about a place called Midway. He had seen some terrible things there, he'd said. Jen tried to remember what they were, and couldn't.

The white-haired old man's eyes rested again on the Enola Gay.

Jen glanced around the museum. Most of her coworkers and the museum's other patrons had gone. She checked her watch and realized the facility was about to close, and she hadn't even seen the gift shop. Adjusting her purse strap on her shoulder, she walked away.

"Beautiful old gal," whispered the old man to the B-29.

In the museum shop, a stack of small boxed models of the Enola Gay caught her attention. Hideous, Jen thought. How can they be so proud of that thing?

She selected a photo of F-16s flying in formation, knowing her boyfriend would like it, and headed toward the two cashiers at the checkout. One clerk's eyes widened; he stared at the other and lowered the volume of the radio on the shelf behind them.

"News just said Paul Tibbets passed away today," said the first clerk.

The second cashier rang up Jen's purchase. "That's sad. I heard him speak when he was here a few years ago. Really interesting stuff."

Jen took her bag and left the shop. Just inside the door stood a book display, an arrangement of hardcover copies of *Sixty Years Later: Reflections on the War,* by Paul W. Tibbets. The sign told her Tibbets was the pilot of the Enola Gay. The cover pictured him standing beside the plane. Jen's feet felt suddenly impossibly heavy; she didn't—couldn't—move from the spot. Something cold and sharp tightened in her gut. Everything around her seemed to disappear, fading as her huge eyes took in only the image on the book. The chill crawled from her stomach, covering her like an icy blanket.

She considered, over the thudding of her heart, going back to say something to the old man, but she knew he wouldn't be there. She knew he had just come to take one last look at his "old gal."

Jen hurried back into the gift shop and bought the book. She might never understand, might never agree with him, but she would read it and learn. She felt she owed him that much.

Of Winter's Curse

Robin Masnick

I never expected to fall in love. After all, I'm a D'Inverno - a descendent from the family "of winter", and my legacy was an ancient one. I must forever bear a cold heart. That's why my mother named me Regina; to create my destiny. I was to become the Queen of Winter.

My eyes blurred with troubled thoughts. I let the letter drift from my hand to the polished oak floor of my Georgetown brownstone; my mind dizzy from trying to conjure a rational explanation.

Curses. A load of crap, wasn't it? I began to pace the floor. This was the twenty-first century; curses were the product of ignorance and Hollywood thrillers. I paused beside the front windows overlooking my busy street, and slid my finger between the mini-blind slats. The late summer's sun sparkled as my fellow 'Washingtonians' hurried past on warm, cobble-stone sidewalks deftly ignoring honking horns, and oblivious to the ornate iron balustrades and decorative brick entryways on each side of the street. Curses belonged in the land of fairytales and campfire stories. I stood back letting the slats snap shut - not here in the modern brilliance of city life.

Except some times, in the deepest night, during those lonely hours where sleep refuses to concede, this modern knowledge did nothing to quell the ancestral fear that Mama cultivated during my entire childhood. Anything seemed possible then.

I shivered and turned away from the window with a sudden need for tea. I gathered the items and decided to have Mama's special, homemade blend. I sunk my nose deep in the canister and relished the scent of crumbled flowers, roots, and stems. I poured water into the kettle, and almost laughed aloud remembering the time when Mama first told me she was a witch - but I choked instead.

"You mean like in the Wizard of Oz? Are you a good witch or bad witch?" My twelve year old self had carefully restrained a bubbling giggle. Mama couldn't possibly be serious, could she?

Mama expelled the well-rehearsed sigh, "Oh, *Regina*"; a sure sign of disappointment when through the years, I failed to understand her subtle hints on topics she never wanted to discuss, such as sex, her past, or my absent father.

"Of course not. But you must beware, and never repeat what I'm about to tell you." Mama's seriousness and force was so uncharacteristic, I nearly froze. "Promise me. This must remain a secret".

What else could I do? I was scared out of my senses; my mother was acting like a lunatic. "Yes, Mama. I know how to keep a secret."

"There are things in this world about which you know nothing about." Mama's face became grim as she searched my eyes. Marked agitation overtook my mother as she absent-mindedly moved about the room in a mock effort of tidying up imaginary clutter. "I never told you about our family, but there's something you need to know for your own protection - and others."

My heart thumped in response to Mama's ominous tone. I had suddenly felt too hot, yet clammy with a cold sweat, and wished with all my might I was anywhere except in this living room. I didn't want to know her crusty old secret, I didn't! "Mama, I promised Pammy that we would do homework together this afternoon, I really –"

Mama stopped midway from swiping the non-existent dust from beneath a vase she was still holding, and turned to stare at me from across the room. She seemed a little shocked, and then I felt the tension leave her as defeat entered. Mama calmly put down the vase and came to kneel before me. Taking my hands, she stared at our joined palms. "I am a witch. As my mother before me and her mother before her." She paused, releasing my hands. "As you are too."

I thought this sealed the deal. My mother had gone batty and the world was quickly sliding into weird. Best thing to do was humor her so I could get out of there and back to the land of homework, friends, and dance recitals. I tried to use the calmest

49

voice possible, like people do on TV when they approach a crazy person. "It's Ok, Mama. I won't tell anyone."

We never mentioned that day again. There were times when my mother seemed excessively strange to me, but I reasoned whose mother doesn't go nuts from time to time? Like when I started getting interested in boys. Mama kept cautioning me, "People like us, can *never* fall in love; and it is our responsibility to make sure that no one falls in love with us. We are D'Inverno's, the family of winter. We must always ensure that our hearts remain cold, or tragedy will strike."

Exactly what tragedy or why we should be so different when people fell in and out of love on a daily basis, she never did say; but I learned over the years that "people like us" was her secret code for "witches" and that my last name D'Inverno was Italian. That at least explained my honey-colored hair, brown eyes, and the fact that I tanned so easily on sunny summer days, perhaps even my predilection for pizza and anything involving pasta.

There was only one time that I could remember, when my mother referred to this odd responsibility as The D'Inverno Curse. It had something to do with Mama's family, who for generations lived in some small, West Virginia town, where it was impossible to outlive the past; whatever that meant. Mama briefly mentioned her fleeing to Washington, D.C. where I could live a normal life, and possibly outrun the curse. I asked about my father. I only had dim memories of a great laughing figure who, to my utmost delight, would toss me into the air and catch me in strong, warm arms; and who mysteriously vanished when I was about three years old. All Mama would say was that he was the love of her life – and nothing could save him.

"What about *your* Mama? How come she doesn't ever come to see me?" The hurt little girl inside me was feeling doubly abandoned.

"It's better for you Regina to have no part of that life, and for me too." And that was that; door shut, case closed.

So being a kid, I naturally chalked all this up to having a Mom who had the occasional crazy moment, because in every other sense, I lived the life of any normal kid with a single, working Mom. I was particularly proud of my mother for being an accomplished registered nurse for one of the largest medical institutions in the Washington, D.C. area. But mostly because Mama bandaged scraped knees and elbows up and down the length of our street, and became the go-to person for neighbors needing home-remedies, or sometimes, just a compassionate ear.

And I just adored the city. If we weren't boating in the canal, we were picnicking by the river. One of our favorite pastimes was strolling by the historic mansions – Mama called it house-porn since the fancy scrollwork and grandiose architectures evoked such intense desire, it was like enticing eye-candy for house lovers and history buffs.

We especially enjoyed going downtown into D.C.. I grew up with museums, book stores, theatres, and all sorts of international foods at my fingertips. I even had Mama's approval to date boys, so long as I kept it casual, and although her consent was usually accompanied with a strict reminder that boys were an "evil temptation to tragedy", I usually let it go in one ear and right out the other. I figured it to be a harmless exaggeration that Moms often relied on when trying to protect their daughters' virtues.

Lost in the past, I took a sip of tea that had grown icy cold. I got up to nuke it in the microwave and noticed the piece of paper on the floor. I reached down and picked up the letter, rubbing my thumb over the family crest imprinted on the fancy vellum paper. The possibilities were just too awful to contemplate. *Can it really be true?* I set it on the kitchen table, warmed up my tea, and took it back to my seat.

I breathed in the soothing herbal steam rising from my cup, feeling its familiar aroma steady my trembling. Glancing at the letter, I thought about my indifference to boys over the years. High school crushes came and went, but I really didn't care about romance anyway because I had so many other interests. Then my college years sped by in a blur of part-time jobs and classes; it became easy to avoid any lasting relationships. By the time I began my career, I knew it was a professional risk to even date where you worked let alone have a serious relationship.

But then I met Jeffrey, and the world stood still.

We first saw each other across the crowded lunch room at work. He was new, just transferring in from another company, and getting the corporate tour. I had been talking with a group of colleagues by the salad bar, when I felt the pull of energy. Startled, I looked around and spotted Jeffrey. He was facing me, watching me, and our eyes locked.

It was like an electrical current opened between our two bodies. The room receded from my vision, all sound faded away, and I became cushioned inside a pale mist. I struggled to break our gaze. I don't think I even smiled a polite hello. The room returned to normal and I quickly glanced back; but it was too late. Never before had I experienced such an intense connection. All of my cautions cracked and crumbled, and like Humpty Dumpty who had a great fall, I tumbled down; wanting more, wanting him.

Days turned into weeks. I had kept my growing relationship secret from not only Mama, but my friends and colleagues as well. I was breaking rules on all fronts.

At the time, I regarded my unusual reticence to share Jeffrey like an act of superstition, lest the knowledge of my growing love thwart the budding romance; but, I was kidding myself.

Eventually Jeffrey began pressuring me about meeting my family and friends. He understood the fine line we walked on at work, but he teased me that I was a woman without a past. I was able to delay things for quite a while, by reasoning that my colleagues and my friends were one and the same. Yet I knew it was only a matter of time before I had to tell Mama. I broke the cardinal rule and committed the unspeakable crime. I had fallen deeply, and truly, in love.

It was exactly six months ago today when I finally told Mama. I had expected a massive guilt trip, or to be scolded for my foolishness, but surprisingly Mama's only words were, "So it will be."

And now Mama was gone. If I had known that a drunk driver would end her life so soon, I would have spared her the disappointment and never have told her about Jeffrey. The letter in front of me grew watery as tears pooled in my eyes. *Mama, I miss you so much. I don't know what to do.*

I pushed the letter aside and grabbed a tissue. Here was another disaster, and I just didn't want to give it credence. I checked the clock, and was shocked that only fifteen minutes had passed since I read my grandmother's letter. Each tick of the second hand seemed to intensify my craving for Jeffrey's soothing embrace, but it was still too early, he wouldn't be able to leave work for another hour.

It was then that I noticed. Outside my kitchen window, it started to rain. Did my tears bring the rain? If I could kill a man by the sheer power of my love, would the clouds share my misery and pour tears of rain in sympathetic sorrow? How ridiculous it all seemed. There were no such things as witches and curses – right?

I glanced once more at the letter and quickly decided there was only one way to find out. I reached for my cell phone and dialed for directory assistance. It was time to meet my grandmother.

Five weeks later, I found myself comfortably seated in an antique chair warming my chilly feet in front of the fireplace, which turned out to be one of many housed within my grandmother's Victorian estate, deep in the lush hills near historic Harper's Ferry, West Virginia. I just came in from spending the day planting white tulip bulbs on my mother's grave in the D'Inverno family plot; anxious for Mama's final resting spot to bloom with her favorite flower once spring arrived. It had been an unseasonably cool autumn day, and even though the sun peeked through grey, misty clouds, a chill wind rattled through dying leaves which sounded like crashing waves of a distant ocean. I was glad to be back in the warmth of my bedroom.

Jeffrey had called repeatedly that day and I felt bone-weary tired. I wondered how long I could continue to put him off; I needed to find a solution soon. I didn't think that breaking off my engagement would be enough to protect him, because it was already too late. I loved him heart and soul.

I had learned a lot these past few weeks, under the expert tutelage of my grandmother. I now understood why Mama ran away in fear and torment. My heart once again swelled with love, thankful for Mama's most precious gift – the chance for me

53

to have a normal childhood, to be far apart from the town gossips, superstitious fear, and children's cruel taunts that generations of D'Inverno women have endured. I also learned the family's most guarded secret.

It was true. I came from a long, ancestral line of Italian witches, called Strega. They emigrated to America in the mid-1800s and settled into a small community in West Virginia, where they profited mostly from inheriting their husbands' estates. An ensuing pattern that didn't escape the townsfolk's attention, and over the years it became clear. The D'Inverno husbands always died within two or three years, after bearing at least one daughter. Rumors began to ripple.

The women were suspected of poisoning their husbands. Fingers pointed to their elaborate herb gardens and tongues wagged about the women's timeless beauty. But no proof could be produced and our women were mostly left alone to live their lives in seclusion.

Except for the desperate souls, the ones who sought them out under the cover of darkness, the folks seeking magic cures for broken hearts and sick bodies alike. My relatives were renowned for their large cupboards, brimming with vials, tins, dark hued bottles, and bags of suspicious, and sometimes foul smelling, substances.

But the *big* secret was the family curse. No one knew how it got started, or which of the Strega was responsible, only that any man a D'Inverno woman truly loved, would meet an untimely death. So the women of winter learned to nurture a cold heart – well, the ones that actually believed in the curse.

I shifted in my chair, noticing steam rising from my wet socks. Three gentle raps sounded on my bedroom door. I called out a welcome and my grandmother appeared in the opened doorway. I jumped up and helped the old woman to the other fireside chair.

I tried to wrap an afghan around her thin legs but she gently pushed me away and frowned, "Oh, don't fuss. I'm perfectly capable of taking care of myself." I stood back and restrained a grin when she settled into the afghan just the same.

"Grandmother, I was looking through the books you loaned me the other day and I had some questions."

"I figured you might. I want you to remember how dangerous some of them can be. You are not to attempt any spells without consulting me first. Do I have your agreement?" My grandmother sat regally on her throne, exuding power and strength.

"Yes, of course. You have my word." I struggled on how to bring up the subject without alarming her.

Satisfied, my grandmother sank back into her chair and contemplated the warm fire. "What is it you want to know?"

"I was thinking about the curse." I sneaked a peak to check for alarm, but she didn't move. "Has anyone ever been able to break it?"

"Of course not! You think we didn't try?" She turned a perplexed eye to me, as if I had temporarily lost my mind, before settling back to enjoying the fire's heat.

"I didn't mean to imply that no one tried; I was just wondering if there was any way to maybe, *avoid* the curse?" I held my breath, so much rested on the answer to this question.

I anxiously waited for Grandmother's reply, but she just continued to stare into the flames and I began to wonder if she even heard my question. I finally had to release my breath, deciding it would be best to wait for her to speak first.

"You could try a Love Spell," she began. "But it would be extremely dangerous, for both you and your man." Grandmother scowled and shifted in her seat. "And it may not work. It may not be worth the price."

"Oh! Um – I don't believe I mentioned a – I didn't intend...", but the lie paused on my lips leaving a nasty taste in my mouth, like spoiled grapes.

"Lies don't taste too good, do they?" She smirked with hidden knowledge. "I'm too old and have seen too much. Of course I know about your man. And you want to save him."

Relief soared through my veins, leaving me limp and ragged. "Yes, more than anything. I love him Grandmother. It's too late. What can I do to protect him?" The clock ticked loudly in the silent room as I waited for the answer.

"When you banish a thing, you must fill its place with something else." My grandmother stared into the dancing flames. "If you don't, the gods will fill it for you." She turned glazed eyes to mine and the fire's burning logs cracked with a loud pop. "And you don't want that."

I shrugged aside the foreboding overtone. "I'll do anything."

Grandmother turned back to the fire, away from my earnest face. She seemed to age a dozen more years in that one brief moment. "Yes, Dearest. I believe you would."

It was dark. A root caught Jeffrey's toe and he stumbled on the forest trail. Two hooded cloaks reached out to catch him from falling. I crossed my fingers, hoping the herbal potion I slipped to Jeffrey earlier that evening would last. With a little luck, and some plausible deniability, he would think this night was only a dream.

The woods were eerie, especially at this time of year. I involuntarily shivered beneath my scratchy wool garment and pulled a tissue to wipe my cold, drippy nose. Grandmother insisted that the spell needed to be performed during the full moon, when the goddess' power was at her greatest. Luckily, it fell near Thanksgiving this month - perfect timing to lure Jeffrey to the wilds of West Virginia. The lie still clung to my lips; poor Jeffrey had been so anxious to finally meet the family of which I had kept so secret.

I could see bits of moon light caught in the web of tree limbs over my head, but the forest was so thick, the misty rays couldn't penetrate far enough to reach the leaf-strewn floor. The path seemed well-traveled to my inexperienced steps, and the overpowering smell of earthy moss, wet bark, and dead leaves enveloped my senses.

"How much further?" I asked the older woman walking behind me. I suddenly felt scared and insecure without my grandmother's strong presence, even though she had reassured me that these people could be trusted. I knew it was her advanced age that kept her from being with me tonight, but I missed her all the same.

The answer came across like a disembodied voice floating out of the darkness. "Almost there."

Maybe I am crazy. Panic began to rise and a ragged breath caught in my chest as I thought about what we were about to do. I felt light-years away from the familiar sights and sounds of Georgetown's busy streets, and the security of my cozy little brownstone.

A man's hand grabbed my shoulder. "It's all right. You and Jeffrey have nothing to fear from us." The small group of travelers paused on the path as the man continued, "But I must ask you one final time - are you *certain* you want to do this? We can turn around right now - no harm done."

I panted to catch my breath; I felt my eyes open wide and look about wildly, trying to discern faces through the inky blackness. Jeffrey was slumped, quietly docile, and supported by muscular arms. I nodded my head, took in a deep breath of chilled air, and held back the cough from its sting. *I have to do this. I need to save him.* "Yes. I'm certain."

Within moments, I could see flickering flames between the trees; it looked like sets of brazen eyes peering out of the darkness. I strained my ears and detected soft singing, but I couldn't hear the words and didn't recognize the song.

The trail ended at the edge of a circular meadow and my heart picked up speed. About a dozen torches burned holes in my vision and the full moon's soft glow blanketed the frosty ground. I followed Jeffrey's form through a ring of hooded figures to a long table covered with a pure white tablecloth. Various objects lay strewn across its surface – candles, a plate with cookies, a wine bottle, and a sharp looking double-edged dagger. The singing stopped.

I was led over to the side of the altar and instructed to sit beside Jeffrey. There was a shallow hole dug in the earth with flowers lying at the bottom. Another figure stepped forward and tipped a brown glass vial past Jeffrey's lips before stepping back to take his place in the outer ring. I huddled beneath my cloak, leaned heavily against Jeffrey's reassuring shoulder, and watched the High Priest and Priestess begin the ritual. Arms held high they invoked the God and Goddess, and others called to the Elemental spirits of Earth, Air, Fire, and Water.

And then it was time.

The High Priest stood in front of me, holding the sharp blade. The High Priestess helped me and Jeffrey kneel and face each other over the flower-strewn pit in the ground. I searched Jeffrey's placid expression, thankful to not see drool, but worried for him just the same. The blade came into focus and my hand was brought high. The High Priest sliced my finger, and I pressed the wound to draw out red, ruby drops of blood. The High Priestess handed me a small cloth doll, its body and face were made of beige cotton, and it wore a calico skirt. I smoothed my blood over the doll's chest; then more across its blank face.

The High Priest repeated the process with Jeffrey's blood across the male doll counterpart and handed it to me. I took a red silk cord, tightly bound the two dolls together, and dropped them into the hole. Just as my grandmother schooled me, I pooled my desire and let it swirl and fill my entire body. With palms turned outward, I raised my arms high into the sky and loudly chanted.

"Bright Lady, Moon Goddess of Love
Lend Your power and strength from above,
Take my Lover's fate far from this Curse
Its bonds I ask you to break and disperse,
Tie us hand to hand and heart to heart
And we shall be and never part."

I took the spade from another cloaked hand, and covered dirt over the bound dolls. Patting the soil firmly as if I was planting a seed, I finished the Spell by speaking the final words.

"My love is stronger than the Curse,
Stronger than our lives,
The earth shall hold my binding will
for Jeffrey to survive."

A shadow covered us and we all turned to watch a smoky blue cloud blot out the moon's face. The High Priest nudged my arm. "You must finish. Finish it now!" I reached for the twin set of candles, one red and one white that had been joined together by running a flame up the side of one candle and pressing it against the other. I quickly spread some of our blood along each of the candles, lit both wicks, and tilted them over the spaded soil to drip a pool of wax that hardened almost upon impact. I sat back on my heels, and sealed the Spell. "So Mote It Be."

Thunder's rumbling growl snarled over our heads. I flinched from its unexpected bark and saw the torches sputter in a sudden gust of wind. Then, like a magician that snapped his fingers, all was quiet.

The moon's face once more bathed us in her soft, evening light and it was time to close out the ritual. I held onto Jeffrey and searched the night sky - silently praying that whatever force controls things such as curses, would see this spell as a universal balance. I was determined to protect Jeffrey from the curse, by binding him with my love.

I paused from writing, my pen held mid-air as I listened to the fierce wind outside my drape-covered windows. The flames sputtered in the fireplace and shadows crept down the faded wallpaper to travel across threadbare carpet.

I shivered with preternatural cold. All these years later, my grandmother's words still echoed in my mind. *You must understand that all magic comes with a price. This Love Spell, it would become an unnatural thing. You would be bound together for eternity. Are you really willing to pay the price?*

I carefully lit the candle with trembling fingers, and then continued writing my note.

...should have listened more carefully to your warning. Jeffrey hounds me day and night; I don't have a moment's peace. How could I have known that he would still lose his life, only to have his spirit tortured, and earthly bound to mine?

I winced from a sensation of fingernails scraping across the back of my neck. I accepted the punishment – waiting it out – and resumed writing.

Please forgive me for what I'm about to do. There is only one way to end his pain, I have to try. Please take care of our daughter. Tell her about my fate when she's old enough to understand. She must never fall in love.

Yours forever, Regina.

I carefully folded the letter and put it into an envelope addressed to my grandmother. I then tilted the burning candle over the flap, and pressed the D'Inverno seal to the warm pool of wax.

I looked up, alarmed at the flickering ceiling light. My bedside lamp flung itself, crashing against the opposite wall, and I covered my face from the splintered glass and metal scattering across the room. Then I cringed from a sudden, sharp pain to my shin; it felt like a swift kick from a heavy boot.

"Ok – Jeffrey. We'll do this your way."

I calmly reached for the vial next to my chair and poured its contents into my steaming cup of tea. I leaned back into my chair, slowly sipping, hoping against hope that the hemlock would work quickly.

"I'll be seeing you soon, my Love".

The empty cup fell with a thud from my weakened hand. I rolled my head to watch the gasping flames, and waited for everything to turn black.

Pickpocket

Judy Gibson

The sound, high-pitched but blessedly short, was broken by a long pause before repeating like a record stuck on the same irritating note. Turning his head left, toward the noise, Pete saw colored lines, two slightly jagged and one with regular spikes, ugly shades of pastel but so bright they seemed to glow, floating there in mid-air. As a shadow moved between him and the lights, Pete sank back into darkness.

When he woke again, even though the room was dark, Pete could tell he was in a hospital. There were metal rails at the side of the bed. Disinfectant stung his nose. A plastic bag, heavy with liquid, hung from a pole, and a tube ran from the bag to a needle in Pete's arm.

He remembered driving, one hand clenching the steering wheel while he honked at the idiot ahead of him. The light had turned yellow, and Pete had jumped lanes, hitting the accelerator to make it through. There had been something heavy and fast, something Pete didn't quite recall. "I was hit." He tried the words on for size. "Some jerkwad hit me." He thought about sitting up, but his body seemed to weigh three times more than it should. The heaviness dragged him back down into sleep.

Underneath the high-pitched beeping was a low rumbling, that of an electric motor. Pete knew the sound. Blearily, he opened his eyes only to wince them shut again. He turned his head away from the light and blinked his eyes open. When he looked around, sunlight was streaming in through the windows, blazing against crisp white sheets. His girlfriend Chelsea, her pink hair peeking out from below a paisley cap, was sitting at the far end of the room. In one hand she held a tube and in the other a small bowl. Water flowed from the tube, into the bowl, and then down into a larger container. Pete knew, from long experience, that a motor was pushing water back up through the tube. As he watched, Chelsea shifted the angle of the bowl to see how it would change the water flow. She was playing with fountains again. When she'd started, during their second year of college, the year he'd shifted his focus from art to business, he'd thought the fountains were a passing fancy. He sank into the bed with a sigh. He'd given up childish things. Why couldn't she?

"Pete?" She was at the side of his bed, looking down at him. "How are you feeling?" Wrapping her fingers around his, she leaned over and brushed a kiss against his forehead. Pulling back slightly, she stared into his eyes.

"What are you doing?" he asked.

"Checking for a concussion." She held up one hand. "How many fingers?"

"What happened?" he asked, although he had a pretty good idea.

"Fingers," she repeated.

"Three," Pete said, knowing she wouldn't answer him until she was satisfied. "Now will you tell me what happened?"

"Your car was hit. Don't you remember?" she asked, sitting on a chair next to the bed.

"Vaguely. I know I was driving," he said. "What about the other car? Was anyone else hurt?"

She shook her head. "No, the other driver was drunk, but he came out of it okay, better than you anyway."

Just my luck, Pete thought. The other guy walks away while I'm stuck in the hospital.

Before Pete could ask how long until he could leave, Chelsea jumped up and brought over a bouquet of flowers. "Your parents sent these. Don't they smell nice?" Pete brushed the flowers away. "And those are from the guys at your job." She nodded toward flowers and a balloon, blue with the words "Get Well Soon" spelled out across.

"Sent?" Pete asked. What, the guys couldn't be bothered to visit? Was Dave too busy bitching about benefits to walk four blocks?

"I told them you weren't awake." Before Pete could reply, she added, "I'll get someone to check on you. Maybe you can make some calls after you've seen the nurse."

Chelsea came back with a young man, a nurse based on his scrubs. Pete couldn't tear his eyes away as the nurse picked up the chart at the foot of the bed. Something sat on the nurse's shoulder. Pete didn't know what it was, but just seeing it made him want to run out of the room. Obviously alive, it was a... a... something. He couldn't come up with a better word for it than creature.

About the size of a mouse, it had a long snout-like nose that never stopped sniffing the air. When it turned toward Pete, he could see that it had no eyes, just slight indentations where eyes should be. Its mouth, a small hole that looked like the barrel of a gun, seemed cold to his sight. The grayish cast of the creature's skin made its long, thin fingers look almost like bones as it pulled something bluish and wispy out of the nurse's hair.

When the nurse came closer, Pete's hand reached out to the nightstand. His fingers wrapped themselves around a pen as if it were a knife. The nurse leaned down, and the creature stretched out toward Pete, its snout sniffing at a furious pace. Pete raised the pen like a weapon. The nurse took a few steps back. "Pete," Chelsea shouted. The creature froze and then vanished. It didn't scamper off and hide. It simply vanished.

"Can I have that?" Chelsea asked over the nurse who was saying, in a soothing voice, that everyone should just keep calm.

Pete looked down and saw he was gripping a pen. With an apology, he handed it over. The nurse, after asking Chelsea if she'd be all right, almost ran for the door.

"What was that thing?" Pete asked.

"Thing?" Chelsea glanced around the room.

"That creature on the nurse's shoulder."

Chelsea scanned Pete's face as if trying to read his thoughts and then dashed out of the room. Her eyes were red when she came back. "I told them to hurry."

When the doctor came in, Chelsea pulled him off to a corner. Pete could hear the occasional word, catching something about hallucinations as he watched another creature – its skin a darker shade of gray than the first one Pete had seen – eating blue gauze it had stretched out of the doctor's head.

Why didn't Chelsea react? Didn't she see it? She was less than two feet away and staring intently at the doctor. Pete blinked and shook his head. The creature was still there. Maybe it was a hallucination. Maybe he was crazy. Pete wished he hadn't said anything about them. He could still do that, pretend he'd stopped seeing them, but if they were a sign of concussion, he should be telling everyone.

The doctor turned his back on Chelsea and walked to the bed. He didn't even raise his eyes from the clipboard as he introduced himself and asked what the problem was. Pete, still not sure if he should mention them or not, described the creature he'd seen on the nurse but didn't say anything about the one the doctor was carrying. The doctor didn't seem concerned, calmly saying they'd run a few extra tests, but that a certain amount of disorientation wasn't uncommon after an impact. As the creature pulled at a sparkling strand of blue gauze, Pete tried to believe it wasn't there.

After the doctor had left, Pete looked out the doorway, watching people as they passed. He winced every time someone with a creature went by, but the people without creatures were almost worse. They allowed Pete to believe, even if only for a moment, that he'd stopped seeing the things.

A few hours after the doctor had seen him, Pete was wheeled out for some type of a scan. When he was brought back, Chelsea wasn't there, but a nurse, a woman this time, was sitting in the chair by his bed. Pete scanned her shoulder, which seemed empty, but he couldn't quite forget that the first creature he'd seen had vanished while he was watching it.

She held out her hand. "Diana McLaren."

Surprised by the warmth of her greeting – the doctor's name had practically gotten lost in the rush of his questions – Pete shook her hand, relaxing in the warmth of human touch. "Peter Teasdale. Pete."

"I heard that you see them," she said.

"I saw," he started to say. He wasn't sure why she was there. Was she checking for a concussion or looking to see if he was mad? "I saw something, shortly after I woke up."

"They're eating," she said. "What they eat is blue, as dark as the sky at twilight but electric. It almost shimmers, stretched out like the Milky Way spread across the night sky."

Pete stared. "How'd you know?"

"You're not the only one who sees them," she said. "Some people can, sensitive we're called, although it's not useful to let people know you can see. It runs in my bloodline, the Sight does, but it was probably your accident that kicked it off for you. It happens that way sometimes. You'll likely keep seeing them, now that you've started."

Wondering if she was putting him on – it sounded like something out of a Stephen King novel – Pete asked, "What are they?"

She leaned in toward him and spoke quietly. "They're called pickpockets; at least that's what I was taught to call them. It's because they're thieves, taking what should be most important to a person."

"What is it they're eating?" He wasn't sure why he was whispering since they were alone in the room.

"You're not going to believe it," she said.

"You're kidding, right? I've been seeing" – he paused to find the right word – "goblins all day. What could be more implausible than that?"

"Souls," she said, leaning in even closer. "They eat souls."

"What?" His retort, loud after their whispering, seemed to ricochet around the room.

She pulled away but continued to speak quietly. "I once knew a man who said he died a bit each day on the way to work. That's not a metaphor. If you aren't passionately living your life, you can start losing bits of your soul. Pickpockets feed off of souls, taking those bits that are loose and eating them."

"But everybody's got one," he said. "Well, not everybody, but I was watching earlier today." He thought back to the people he'd seen. "Three out of four had pickpockets, that's what I saw." He started speaking quickly, as if talking faster would make his words true. "It's because we're in a hospital, isn't it? The suffering and pain, it draws the pickpockets." When she shook her head, he added, "It can't be like this everywhere."

"So many people don't love their lives."

"You don't have one." His words sounded like an attack, even to his own ears.

"My family lives nearby, in a big old house in Herndon, the one I grew up in, and I'm over there every weekend. I share a townhouse with a couple of friends, one my best buddy, a girl I've known since kindergarten. And I love my job. Working in obstetrics, bringing new lives into the world, is exhilarating. Babies have so much potential, the whole world opening up to them."

Pete thought about his own workdays, spent listening to John's latest obsession, which seemed to change almost weekly, or to Dave's latest complaint, which changed just as often. He shook his head. "Your life can't be perfect."

"I never said that." She sat silently for a moment. "About two years ago my fiancé died."

When she didn't say anything else, Pete told her he was sorry.

She shook her head. "Thanks, but it was a while back. My point is that everyone's life is full of both joys and sorrows. The highs and lows aren't the issue. It's the day-to-day drudgery that kills your soul."

"And that lets pickpockets eat them?"

She nodded a yes.

"What's it do?" Pete asked. "This soul sucking, what's it do to a person?"

"Have you ever wondered why children are so joyful, so full of life, while some old people are so miserable they drain the life out of everyone around them?"

"That's it?" Pete asked. "Pickpockets make old people grumpy?"

Diana shook her head. "Without a soul, you'd have no joy, no creativity, no *life* in your life."

"So you'd have a regular, normal life. So what?"

Diana leaned forward and grabbed Pete's hands. "It's not a normal life. It's not what life should be." She stared at him intently and then sighed. "When I was in college I saw a performance, a scene where the actors sat and stared at a TV, never taking their eyes off the screen. It's a bit of an exaggeration, but that's what life is like without a soul."

"Television is the opiate of the masses?" Pete asked.

"Or alcohol. Or valuing money or property more than people. Or any of a thousand other things."

Pete waved away what those other things might be. "Why'd you tell me this?"

"I heard about your hallucinations, or what the doctor is calling hallucinations. I knew what they really were."

"And?" Pete asked.

66

"You've got a choice."

"I could stop seeing them?" Why hadn't she led with that?

Diana jumped in her seat, as if his words had startled her. "No, what I meant was you could take it as a sign, a signal that you need to change your life. Do what you love to do, and you'll be all right."

"Oh," he said, raising one hand like a late-night TV preacher. "God has laid His hand upon me. Son, you are healed. Go and sin no more."

When Diana stood and said she had to get back to work, Pete was surprised. He hadn't meant to drive her away; that usually took a lot more snark. Diana took two steps toward the door, stopped, and turned back toward Pete. "I hope you'll be all right." With that she was gone, out of the room and presumably down the hall before he could even think to ask what she'd meant by that.

Pete felt as if he'd missed a connection, but couldn't think why. He wasn't even sure he believed her, although there was something off about the – he might as well call them pickpockets. It wasn't as if he had a better name for them. He wondered why some people had them while others, like Chelsea, didn't. Diana would say that Chelsea loved her life, but studying art and playing around with fountains, that wasn't a life, that was kid's stuff. Pete had done the same thing, and yeah, he'd loved drawing, or thought he had at the time, but he'd grown up.

He felt relieved when Chelsea came in to tell him he was being released that afternoon. They chatted on about nothing much at all, stuff Pete couldn't even recall five minutes later, until he was allowed to leave. As Chelsea drove him home, Pete noticed the pickpockets. They were everywhere. Not everyone carried one, but most people did.

Chelsea pulled up to his townhouse but didn't get out of her car, saying she needed to get back to her schoolwork. Pete knew he should reassure her, let her know he was okay, but he couldn't bring himself to say the words.

As Pete dawdled over leftover Chinese, his cellphone rang, playing out Dave's tone. Pete looked at the cell but didn't answer. The guys must want him to go out drinking. While a beer, or ten, didn't seem like a bad idea, Pete knew he'd see the pickpockets. Sure his friends wouldn't have any, but the pickpockets would be there. It was just simple statistics: someone in the bar would be carrying one, and Pete wasn't ready to deal with it. "Tomorrow," he muttered as he clicked off the ringer. Pete crawled under his covers and fell asleep.

His dreams were a series of nightmares, jumbled images with no rhyme or reason, nothing connecting one to the other. Mud grabbed at his boots, holding him fast. He reached out for the merry-go-round horses as they bounded away, faster than he could follow. In a dark and narrow room, the walls drew in closer as he slammed against them, trying to break free. Strips of cloth wrapped themselves around him, holding his bound limbs still, pulling tighter, drawing the breath out of him. Pale faces barked conflicting orders; he tried to obey but nothing made any sense. The words weren't even words, not in any language he'd ever heard, and the voices didn't even sound human. Pete bolted up in his bed and glanced wildly around the room until he identified the sound as jazz pouring out of his clock radio.

Blindly, his eyes barely open, Pete stumbled into the bathroom. After he'd started the shower, he felt more than saw his way into the kitchen for a cup of coffee. By the time he was awake enough to shower, the bathroom was full of steam. Shaving, having to feel for the stray hairs, was harder than he'd expected, but he didn't feel like wiping down the mirror. Not hungry, he skipped breakfast, dressing for work and getting out the door as quickly as possible. Since his office was within walking distance, Pete set off on foot.

Across the main drag and one block further down, there was a park that had been a parking lot when Pete had moved in. When he'd been house hunting, the parking lot had been a selling point, a place for his friends to leave their cars. Pete hadn't appreciated the transition. The park, mostly cement and stone, had seemed like a waste of space until one spring day when he and Chelsea had brought their gelatos over to the fountain and watched the kids play. Instead of one of those massive sculptural fountains, this was about two dozen spouts set into the cement with water bubbling up, here for a moment and then there for a few minutes, in a pattern too complex for Pete to predict.

"Come on in," Chelsea had said, jumping in to join the kids. Pete had wanted to play but felt awkward, as if it wasn't quite something he should be doing, and had sat on the side, laughing but resisting all attempts to drag him into the fountain.

With a shake of his head, Pete continued toward the office, which was less than a half-dozen blocks away. He closed his eyes before pushing through the revolving doors. "Hey, look who came back." The voice belonged to a security guard, a guy who was friendly with everyone. Pete clenched his hands into fists before looking up, but the guard didn't have a pickpocket. In that cool room, surrounded by steel and plastic and fake wood, relief, as warming as the sun, surged through Pete. Safe, I'm safe here. If the guard was all right, then surely Pete's friends would be.

Pete was in the elevator and about to push the button when a voice called out, "Hold it." The two women who joined him each had a pickpocket. Pete moved to the back of the elevator and tried to ignore them. The taller woman, obviously continuing their conversation, sang out, "Shopping!" Unable to block her out completely, Pete half-listened as she ran on about buying furniture until the women got off on the fifth floor.

Up on the seventh floor, Bob was making a pot of coffee. Pete ducked into his office before Bob could turn and spot him. It wasn't that Bob had a pickpocket. He didn't. It was that Bob found management fascinating. Getting cornered could mean listening to him ramble on about business theory for a good half-hour.

Pete opened his e-mail so he'd look busy, and had read about a dozen messages before he was interrupted. "Hey buddy." It was Dave, who shared an office across the hall with Raj. Pete knew he was grinning like a fool but didn't care. He'd missed these guys. "We tried to call but couldn't get through," Dave added. "Something wrong with your phone?"

As Pete turned to face them, Raj said, "We heard about the accident. How are you feeling?"

Pete cringed in his chair. From Raj's shoulder, a gun-barrel of a mouth was aimed straight at him. On Dave's shoulder, bone-like hands stretched out electric blue strands as if playing a demented game of cat's cradle.

"Are you sure you shouldn't be at home?" Raj's words

sounded distant, as if he were speaking in another room. Pete's feet drew him forward, past his friends, and down the hall. He didn't want to go but couldn't stop himself. He pushed open the bathroom door. Three steps took him to the mirror.

Pete looked up. He could see it in the mirror, sitting right there on his shoulder: the eyeless face, the twitching snout, the gray skin, the bone-like fingers full of blue gauze.

With a scream, Pete slapped at his shoulder. The pickpocket vanished. Pete couldn't feel it, but he knew it was still there. He scrambled out the door and ran down the hall. There was someone by the elevators. Blindly, Pete felt for the stairwell door. His feet pounded down the stairs. In the echoes that bounced off the walls, he imagined someone following. At the ground level, he shoved the door shut behind him before anything could get out. Without thinking, he bolted right. Dashing across the street, he barely noticed the screech of tires or the shouted insults. He kept running: past the shops, past the park, and past the condos. At his own door, Pete fumbled with the keys, dropping them once before he was inside.

Pete ran into the bathroom. He looked in the mirror but couldn't see the pickpocket. He knew it was there. With one foot pushing against the wall, he yanked at the towel rack. It didn't budge. He pulled at it again, wrenching the bar five more times until the rack fell apart. Pete threw the bar into the mirror. It scratched the glass. He grabbed the bar and jabbed it into the glass until the mirror lay in shards.

Blue flashed in the few shards that hadn't fallen. Pete fell to the floor and sat there, staring into space. He could feel a long stream – no no no no no – ready to pour out. He slammed his fist into the wall until the plaster was cracked and his hand was bleeding. He stared at the blood. When the phone rang, he threw it at the tiled wall. Pieces of phone fell into the tub. He felt cold, as if he'd been sitting there for hours. Even though he was alone, he heard Diana's voice, her words from the hospital: do what you love and you'll be all right.

He stood and slowly walked up the stairs. In a closet were a couple of boxes from college. He rummaged through until he'd found a colored pencil set and a sketchbook, unused since the summer after he'd graduated.

Not paying attention to what he was doing, Pete sketched aimlessly. He wondered if it would help. When he looked down, he'd drawn a pickpocket. Pete dropped the sketchbook and scurried backward, on his hands and knees, until he hit a wall. The image had landed face up. Pete leaned forward until his hands were on the sketchbook. He tore at the page until the pieces looked more like confetti than a drawing.

When Pete picked up the sketchbook again, it was with the air of a drowning man clinging to a raft. With a gray pencil tracing lightly on the page, he sketched the fountain, nine spouts in the cement with water flowing up from three of them. He drew himself dancing in the spray.

The Last Post

George A. Crawford

The morning mist lent an ethereal quality to the ferry landing. Before the sun came up, it was a place where people's eyes played tricks on them. The locals talked of apparitions who appeared on the banks of the river in the half light of dawn or twilight. But most folks disregarded such fanciful stories.

Annabelle tightened her fingers around the cane pole, careful to avoid the fishhook fastened at the bottom. She tiptoed down the weathered concrete toward the ferry.

"Where ya goin'?" Abigail called out.

"None of your beeswax," Annie shot back. Her plan was foiled. She had hoped to sneak out before her six-year old sister noticed.

"Mommy," Abbie howled, "Annie won't take me with her!"

"Annabelle, take your sister with you!"

"Aw, mom... do I have to?"

"Yes, you have to. And make sure she doesn't fall in the river!"

"Yes ma'am. C'mon, Abbie! If you don't keep up, I'll leave you behind."

"If you do, I'll tell mom."

"You'd better not..."

Annabelle walked as briskly as her legs would carry her toward the old concrete landing.

"Wait up!" Abigail protested. "Mom said you have to take me!"

Annabelle stopped walking and let out a huff, glaring at her little sister. She folded her arms and tapped her foot on the concrete to emphasize the terrible delay Abbie had imposed on her plans. When Abigail caught up, Annabelle took her hand firmly, dragging her down the boat ramp toward the water.

"Stand here until Pa calls for us. Stay away from the water!"

The old Army barge crept toward the landing at White's Ferry. The *General Jubal A. Early* was the first public ferry service on the Potomac River, and the only ferry still running. *Jubal* and her predecessors had carried passengers across the river between Virginia and Maryland since the 1700s. Her steel ramp scraped along the concrete as the ferry nestled up to the landing.

"Hey, sprout! What's going on?" John Foster threw open the metal gate, winding a chain around a cleat to secure the ferry to the landing.

"We're goin' fishin'" Annabelle said. She paused for a moment, considering her next words. Finally, she confided to her father, "Mama said I had to bring Abbie."

"Oh, so that's how it is, hmmm?"

"Yeah," Annabelle's brow furrowed. She brightened suddenly. "Pa, would you take us over to the other side?"

"Let me think about that..."

"Please? Please Papa?"

Abigail chimed in. "Pleeeeaase?"

"Well, do you think you're mature enough for interstate travel?"

"What?"

"Will you watch after your sister?"

"I promise!"

"I suppose there's no harm in it. Hop aboard. Stay near the railing."

Annabelle and Abigail leaned on the railing as the ferry crossed the river. Both watched the rusted cable rise out of the water and pass through the pulleys, straining against the current to ensure the *Jubal* remained on course toward the opposite shore. As the ferry ramp scraped onto the Virginia landing, the sisters had no idea that the national capital was abuzz with activity a mere thirty miles downstream from their tranquil transit.

"Give me a kiss, my sweets," John commanded. He knelt to wrap his arms around his daughters, squeezing them close for a moment. "All right then. Off with you both. Be careful near the water, and watch your footing. The rain made those rocks slippery. Stay where I can see you, all right?"

73

"Okay, Pa. Thanks for the ride."

"Catch a catfish for me!"

The two girls scrambled off of the ferry onto the grassy riverbank. Both leaned against a tree trunk, waving to their father as the *Jubal Early* returned toward the Maryland shore.

"C'mon, I know where we can catch some fish." Like an acrobat on a tightrope, Annabelle held out the cane pole for balance as she negotiated the steep slope. She moved deliberately, grasping tree branches and searching intently for her next hand and foothold.

"Be careful Abbie," Annabelle warned. "Pa was right. It's really slick over here."

She froze when she heard the splash.

"Annie!" Abigail cried out as her head disappeared below the brown water.

"Abbie? Abbie!" Her sister was gone, the ripples spreading against the tree limbs and leaves that were being carried along the shore by the rapid current.

"Pa! Help me!" Annabelle cried as her eyes searched the water. She saw the ferry on the other side. Her father was preoccupied, guiding a line of cars as they descended the ramp toward the steel deck.

Annabelle suddenly caught sight of Abigail's pink dress and watermelon slice collar. She'd been carried down the river. Abbie didn't raise her head.

"Help me! Somebody help! Anybody! She'll drown!"

Annabelle ran down the bank to a point ahead of her sister. She held out the cane pole in hopes that her sister could grasp the other end. If she could only reach out a few more inches. She stretched as far as she dared to reach her sister's hand. One more inch. She stood on her toes, lost her footing, and plunged into the current, taking in a mouthful of the muddy water. Choking, Annabelle fought to keep her head above water and tried to cry out for help.

He appeared out of nowhere, splashing into the water up to his chest. The young man reached out and pulled Abbie's limp body toward him, lifting her head clear of the murky water. With his other hand, he took firm hold of Annabelle's shoulder, pulling her to the shore and laying her across a large rock.

74

Grasping at a low hanging branch, he pulled himself and Abbie out of the river. He scrambled barefoot up the riverbank.

Annabelle was horrified at her little sister's dull pallor.

"Come on, girl. Breathe!" the stranger demanded in a deep voice, strands of sandy brown hair brushing in front of his eyes. He sat on the grass, laid Abbie across his worn blue wool trousers, and lifted her arms above her head. "Spit that water out of your tummy! Come on, now."

After what seemed an eternity, Abbie coughed. The color flushed back into her face. She started to cry.

"There you go, little one. Just rest yourself for a bit. You'll be right as rain directly. Lands o' Moses, you're soaked through! Did you think you were a duck?"

Abbie stopped crying and looked at her rescuer.

"That must be it, then. I shall call you 'Baby Duck.' Does that suit you?"

Abbie laughed.

"Thank you, mister," Annie sputtered, trying to spit the grainy mud taste from her mouth. "You saved her."

"Only because I heard your call. It was you who really saved this one. And who might you be, young lady?"

"I'm Annabelle Foster."

"Heavens me! If that isn't a proper name for a lady, then I've never heard one. It's a pleasure to make your acquaintance, Miss Annabelle."

"You talk funny, mister."

"And a spirited young lady at that. How old might you be to conduct yourself with such familiarity?"

"I'm twelve."

"I would have thought you were twenty if you were a day. Are your parents about? It's certain that you two should not be out without a proper chaperone."

"Our Pa is on the other side of the river. He's the ferry master."

"In that event, I shall attend you until he returns. Allow me to introduce myself, Miss Annabelle. I am Joshua Freemantle, Private of the 15th Massachusetts. And how shall I address my new Baby Duck?"

"I'm Abbie," she coughed.

"I confess that I prefer 'Baby Duck,' Miss Abbie. Have we extracted all of the water from your saturated frame?"

"What?"

"Have you expelled the river from your lungs, girl?"

She coughed again. "I think so."

"I'm so glad you were here, Mister Freemantle," Annabelle offered.

"Joshua, sugar plumb. The years between us are not sufficient for such formality."

"Joshua. But I didn't see you earlier. How did you find us?"

"Well, little Miss, we were on a reconnaissance toward Leesburg, when I heard you cry out."

"Recon-a-what?"

"We were ordered to conduct a demonstration to determine the Rebel positions."

"Oh. I'm just glad you heard us. You came so fast."

"I have sisters at home just about your age. When I heard your call, I suspect I imagined you were they for a spell. Naturally, I came running."

"Do you live around here, Joshua? Maybe your sisters can come over and play with us..."

"I regret that they are several days distant. I have not seen them since my fifteenth year, when I signed on with Colonel Devens. Otherwise I am certain they would welcome your kind invitation. Perhaps when this war is over, and you are a bit older, we shall call on you. That is, with your father's permission, of course."

"I'm sure you can ask him. He's probably at the landing by now."

"Before I meet him, permit me to present a token of my affection, Miss Annabelle. If you think me uncustomarily forward, I beg your indulgence. Our futures are uncertain, and we must take advantage of what time we have." Joshua unfastened the top three brass buttons on his dark blue tunic, and reached inside his red and white checkered shirt. He withdrew a small metal medallion. A leather lace had been threaded through a hole punched in the medallion. He lifted it over his head, holding it out for Annabelle to see.

"This fine metalwork was once a Reb Minie' ball that ricocheted off of my belt buckle. I resolved that I should keep that which the Rebs so clearly intended for me. I consider myself most fortunate that the good Lord saw fit to deliver me from its effect. Our blacksmith is a fine craftsman. He flattened it on his anvil, and stamped my name into its surface. I have worn it ever since that day. I surmised that, if I should fall on the field of battle, a friend might recognize me and send a letter to my family. But today I would like you to have it, so that I can tell my compatriots that I have a lady friend who is waiting for me."

Annabelle cooed as he placed the amulet around her neck. "Thank you, Joshua. No one ever gave me a necklace before."

"It's high time someone did." Joshua smiled at her. He blushed suddenly, clearing his throat.

"Well, Baby Duck, you seem to have dried out some. Still, it is probably time to get you to a warm fire. Let me collect my things, and we shall see you to your father."

Joshua helped Abbie to her feet, straightened her dress, and trotted up the hill. He returned with a haversack, a pair of hobnail boots and an ancient, muzzle-loading rifle. The bayonet, affixed to the barrel, glistened in the sunlight.

"I mustn't leave my weapon unattended. Colonel Devens would lash me with a knotted plow line were I to misplace it. It is one of the new Springfield models, you see. I am but one of a few who managed to obtain such a fine piece. When I return home, I shall use it to hunt deer in the woods near our farm."

"You kill the deer? But they're so peaceful and pretty..."

"Yes, Miss Annabelle, I do. God has seen fit to bestow bounty on these rich lands. I believe it was His intention that we should take them for our nourishment. But it is just as important that we should do so mercifully, each taking only that which is needed for one's own sustenance. And we must always be thankful for His blessings. I hope this does not trouble you too deeply. I would feel most accursed and sorrowful if I offended your sensibilities."

"I don't like it. But I understand. Pa hunts, too. And our Ma cooks it. I like her Sloppy Joes the best."

"Sloppy what?"

"You never had a Sloppy Joe, Joshua? What planet were you born on?" It was then that Annie spied her father.

John Foster froze when he saw his daughters. Regaining his senses, he sprinted the hundred yards from the ferry to the girls.

"I thought I told you to keep her clear of the water."

"I tried, Pa, but she slipped off the bank. If it wasn't for Joshua, I don't know what I would've done. He saved her life."

"Who?"

"I'd like you to meet Joshua, Papa. Joshua, this is my fa…" Annie turned, but Joshua was gone. She shouted his name several times, to no avail.

"Annabelle, did you hurt your head? There's no one else here, darling."

"But he was just here, Papa! We were talking about how he hunted deer on his farm back home."

"Well, clearly he didn't want us to see him. We don't have time to linger. We need to get you both home right now. She's damned near drowned. I'm just glad you're both safe. But we're all going to catch hell from your mother."

They rode the ferry back to Maryland in silence. The girls shivered under the wool blankets her father pulled from the emergency kit.

Their mother panicked on catching sight of them. Her anger quickly turned to concern about her children. Annabelle told her mother what had happened as she bathed Abbie.

"Sweetheart, I'm not sure what you saw. We all handle stress in different ways. Your father said that there was no one else around when he saw you. Maybe this Joseph…"

"Joshua, Mama."

"Joshua. I'm sorry. Maybe this Joshua…well, baby…maybe you thought him up because you didn't know what to do. Maybe Joshua is like an imaginary friend, who helped you pull your sister out of the river when no one else was there to help."

"He's not my imagination, mother! I'll prove it. Look! He gave me this necklace!" Annabelle reached inside her dress for the amulet.

Her mother recoiled. "Where on Earth did you get that nasty thing! Take it off your neck this instant!"

"But mom…" Annabelle reached for the necklace. Her hand grasped clay, moss and rotting leather. Annie squealed.

"Here, put that swamp thing into a paper towel, and get out of that dress. You've got mud and grunge all around your neck! Hop into the tub with your sister."

Both girls were soon clean and into fresh pajamas. They sat at the kitchen table, sipping tea, as their mother prepared dinner. Though her mother wanted to push this morning's events into the distant past and return to normalcy, Annabelle did not intend to be dismissed.

"So, you saw the necklace."

Her mother did not respond.

"You saw it, didn't you, Mama?"

"I saw nothing of the sort. That matted bramble you had around your neck could have been anything. Anyway, it's now where it belongs. In the trash."

"What! You threw it away?" Annabelle ran to the waste basket, rummaging through vegetable peelings and coffee grinds until she retrieved a muddy paper towel.

"It's not that you didn't believe me," Annabelle protested. "It's that you don't want to believe me."

"It's nothing of the sort. You just imagined it, that's all." Her mother continued to peel potatoes, avoiding eye contact.

"I'll prove I was telling the truth," Annabelle announced. "Then you'll have to believe me." She took the paper towel to the sink, sidling up next to her mother. She opened the wadded paper towel and placed its contents under the running faucet. Her mother's quick strokes with the potato peeler slowed as the water gradually beat away the clay and moss to reveal a timeworn metal disc. Rotted leather fed through a small hole punched near the top of the disc.

The potato peeler stopped.

"My God," her mother exclaimed. "It is a pendant of some sort. It looks homemade."

"I told you, it's a necklace. But it was brand new this morning. I don't understand what happened."

79

"Let's put it into a box. It looks like it could disintegrate at any minute. Go into my room. There's a little jewelry box on my nightstand. Put this into it. Then we'll have your granddad take a look at it."

"It's a kind of dog tag," Jacob Foster murmured as he held a magnifying glass up to the disk after dinner. "Except that, during the Civil War, the soldiers didn't have dog tags. Some of them would write their address on a piece of paper, and pin it to their uniform. Some would sew their names onto a patch of cloth. Others would write last letters to home, and keep it in a pocket. Still, other made their own dog tags, using wood or metal. They'd carve or stamp their names into the metal, and wear it around their necks. It was the invention of the dog tags, and the Army started issuing them after the war. I'll have to ask an old friend to be sure, but I'm pretty sure what our darling Annabelle has discovered here is a Civil War dog tag."

"But he gave it to me today, granddad."

"Annabelle! What did I tell you this afternoon?" Her mother was becoming exasperated with disbelief. "Sometimes our minds play tricks on us. This was just a trick."

"No it wasn't!" Annabelle was adamant.

"Don't you talk back to me, young lady, or you'll spend tomorrow in your room!"

"Angela, have you considered that Annabelle might be telling you the truth?" Jacob Foster's blue eyes peered over his bifocals at his daughter-in-law.

"Dad, it's just not possible. I mean a Civil War soldier alive in the Virginia woods? Please."

"Well, rather than immediately dismiss the child's account, let's pause for a minute and see if there's something that would make Annabelle's story makes sense. For example: there was a reenactment of the Balls Bluff battle recently."

"I didn't know that. So you think one of the reenactors saved Abigail?"

"Well, I'm just exploring alternative hypotheses. If it had been a reenactor, is it likely he'd have given away a real artifact like this? Why not a replica?"

"I don't know, Dad."

"So, perhaps there's another explanation?"

"Like what, Dad?" John Foster recognized the signals. His father had an idea that he was about to share.

"Before I retired, I spent fifty years crossing that river on that ferry. In the early morning, or late at night, with fog on the river or mist in the trees... well, the light can play tricks on your eyes. You can see things. At least half a dozen times, I swore I saw soldiers standing on the banks of the river. Sometimes, they'd smile and wave. Others, would challenge us. But we always dismissed it as a trick of the light."

"Come on, Dad..."

"You can ask the other pilots. They've seen 'em too."

"Old boatman's talk..."

"You've seen them too, haven't you son?"

John Foster paled. "This can't be happening."

"What are you saying, Dad?" Angela Foster put an arm on her husband's shoulder, looking at her father-in-law in disbelief.

"Tell her, son. The story you told me when you were Annabelle's age..."

"What's he talking about, John?"

"I can't honestly remember much of it clearly... it happened so long ago. I was working the ferry with Dad. It was evening...the sun had just gone down. There was fog along the river. In fact, I'm not even sure now that I saw it..."

"Saw what?"

John was quiet.

"What did you see, John?"

"I thought I saw some soldiers."

"Soldiers?"

"Not just a soldier, was it?" Jacob encouraged his son.

"No... it was a group of young men, dressed up like Union soldiers in the Civil War....you know, the dark blue coats, backpacks, and those little hats with the bill, like they sell at the battlefields? They had long rifles, with those long sword-like bayonets fixed on the tips. They were running from something, tumbling down the hill. Some of them threw their rifles, and dived into the river. Others landed on top of them. Many panicked and seemed to drown. Except for one. He stood on the bank, with his rifle in hand. He turned and looked straight at me… and then he was gone."

The room was quiet.

"Annabelle, would you repeat what you said to me earlier? What did Abby's rescuer say he was doing?"

"He was wrecking something, I think."

"Wrecking?" Her grandfather looked down with a patient smile. "Or reconnaissance?"

"Yeah. That's what Joshua said…"

"What else did he say to you?"

Annabelle's brow furrowed as she tried to recall her conversation with Joshua. "He's not from around here, grandpa. He said his home was a few days away. Joshua said Colonel Devens would be mad at him for leaving his rifle. Oh, and he's private for the fifteenth."

"I wish you wouldn't encourage this, Dad."

"You need to have more faith in your daughter, Angela.

"In October 1861 General McClellan's army fought a battle over by Harrison's Island. You've heard about Balls Bluff? The battle was fought in this area, over by Edwards Ferry. Not a mile from this very spot. A company of the 17th Mississippi surprised a Union infantry regiment, the 15th Massachusetts Infantry, as they tried to cross the river. Many of the Federal soldiers were gunned down in the river. Many more drowned. All told, the Union lost about a thousand men not far from where we're sitting in the comfort of your dining room table--a fourth of them shot or drowned. They say the bodies floated down the Potomac for a week…some as far as Mount Vernon. Over two hundred deaths in one afternoon is a lot of souls for heaven to take.

"In those days, it took several days to get to Massachusetts by horse or wagon. Trains were a bit faster, but expensive. And I believe the commander of the 15th Massachusetts Infantry was one Colonel Devens.

"I can't tell you what to believe, Angela. But I believe our dear Annabelle is telling the truth. And I think I can prove it if you will find me a pencil and a piece of paper."

Annabelle trotted to her room and returned with the items her grandfather requested. He took the medallion, placed it onto the hardwood table, and covered it with the paper. He rubbed the pencil lead gently over the medallion, producing an image of the medallion on the paper's surface. Jacob held the magnifying glass up to the rubbing. He smiled slightly, and handed the rubbing to Annabelle. The paper-white letters stood out against the blue pencil lead:

JOSHUA ABSALOM FREEMANTLE
PVT 15 MASS INF

"You may draw whatever conclusions you wish. But one thing is clear: Annabelle is no storyteller." He smiled at his granddaughter, and took her hand. "Tomorrow, my dear, we are going to walk over to the other side of the river see if we can find your friend Joshua."

They were startled by the splat... splat... splat sound on the door, as if someone were throwing mud pies at the surface.

"It's those darned hooligans again," John Foster murmured, reaching for the doorknob. "Can't they leave a family in peace? I swear, I'm going to get those troublemakers if it's the last thing I..."

He opened the door suddenly to reveal a six-foot mound of mud and moss. Green and brown liquid spattered on the landing. They stared open-mouthed at the somehow familiar form, unsure of themselves, when the mound moved toward the door.

"Greetings and felicitations on this warm summer's eve, sir," a liquid voice gurgled. The form bowed slightly, an appendage gesturing as if tipping a hat. "Do I have the pleasure of addressing Mister Foster?"

"Y..y...yes... I am John Foster." He thought he could make out the shape of a decaying hand, reaching for a rotted slouch cap.

"Good evening, sir," the aqueous voice continued, the words carefully articulated and unmistakable to all in the room. "I am Joshua Freemantle. With your permission, I wanted to call on you to inquire if your daughters are in the mood for an evening stroll?"

Joshua shook his head slightly. Matted layers of decay fell away from his face. Angela fainted as he continued.

"I am most sorrowful that I wasn't able to respond more swiftly this morning. If only I had arrived a moment sooner, I might have saved the young ladies…"

"What do you mean, 'if only'?" Jacob Foster demanded. "Why, the girls are just fine…" Jacob's chest tightened as he felt Annabelle's hand, cold clammy and damp in his grasp. He turned slowly, not wanting look down.

"It's all right, granddad…" Annabelle's faded yellow eyes looked lovingly at Jacob from beneath the matted hair. "It didn't hurt at all. We had to come and say goodbye. Joshua wouldn't have it any other way. We'll be all right. He will watch over us now.

"Abby, Joshua has come for us. It's time to go."

Abigail's feet left small puddles on the tile floor as she struggled against the onset of rigor mortis. She turned back to face them as she reached the doorframe.

"Don't worry about us, Papa." Water seeped over her blue lips. "We don't feel the cold any more. And Joshua will take good care of us…"

"You can be assured of that, child." Joshua held out mossy hands, taking the girls' outstretched arms.

"No," John muttered softly. Jacob collapsed onto the sofa, into the dampness where moments before he had shown Abigail the pendant rubbing.

"I regret that we must be on our way," Joshua bubbled. "Don't despair, sir. I give you my solemn oath that I will look after them."

They staggered slowly into the night, arms intertwined.

The ferry crossing is an eerie place before the sun rises. The locals say that in the morning, before the fog lifts, some have seen a young soldier clad in Federal blue, walking hand-in-hand with two young girls, as if on their way to a picnic. Then again, most folks disregard such fanciful stories.

84

The Nest

Susan Basso McCauley

Sara glanced in her rear view mirror. Dust billowed and then swirled closed upon the pre-Civil War era homes that lay behind her. She stopped beneath a canopy of giant oak trees, their leafy branches dotting the dirt lane with rustling shadows. She double-checked the piece of paper on which she'd written the address, then looked out her window. This was the house.

She turned off the engine. The air conditioner blew out one last breath, and then died. She opened the car door, listening intently before stepping into the summer heat.

The gentle rustle of leaves overhead filled the silence, and somewhere in the branches above she heard the chirping of young chicks waiting to be fed. She squinted up at the sun-dappled tree, trying to see the nest. The sun was bright, hot, but the heat was dulled in the demulcent shade.

She took a deep breath of country air, and gathered her notebook and purse from the front seat. It was so relaxing to get away from D.C., even for an afternoon.

She walked toward the front of the house, but the main door was sealed off and she could find no entrance. She wandered to the back where a white picket fence enclosed the yard. It had no gate, but a large opening between two posts led into the backyard.

The back garden was lush with greenery, silent except for a fountain that trickled eerily into murky water. Slow steps took her down a narrow dirt path toward the backdoor. A swirl of gnats whirled in a ray of sunlight, swarming annoyingly as if devouring some unseen decay.

Sara gazed at the house. Her grandmother had lived in a similar Victorian Gothic in Fairfax. She'd loved that place as a child. Her grandmother's home. It was the first house she'd had to liquidate and sell. Such a sad time. At least her grandmother had already passed.

Sara fought away the feelings of guilt that gnawed at her insides. It was as if she were some sort of reaper. She hoped this old woman was prepared to lose her possessions. She sighed. It had to be done. And if she didn't do it, someone else would. At least she would take a fair cut, not like some of her less reputable colleagues.

She let her unsettling thoughts drift away on the warm summer breeze and walked to the wooden porch that hugged the periphery of the house. The white paint on the walls and warped floorboards was cracking and peeling from age and humidity. Several layers of paint, similar colors, but no clear matches caked the walls.

The humidity pressed in on her as she approached the rickety steps into the shade of the house. The rear door was open, except for an old screen door that hung lopsided from one of its hinges. This place had been loved, even if it was now in ill repair.

From somewhere inside a low moan reached her ears. Perhaps it was an old air conditioner, spluttering through the musty summer heat. Perhaps.

"Hello?" she called through the darkened door.

"I'm Bob," came a man's voice, startling her from behind. He had a slight, Southern drawl, and tilted his hat to her, revealing his salt and pepper hair. "We spoke on the phone."

"Sara Talbot," she said, shaking his hand.

"My wife owns a small antique shop in town. Didn't really feel up to handling what we've got here. Thought you'd be the best."

Sara smiled. "Tell her thank you."

"Will do," Bob said, adjusting his hat.

"Do you live here?" she asked.

"Me? No. Just my Aunt Alta, Great Aunt. The wife and I live just down the road."

She guessed the man was in his late 50s, and if Alta was his Great Aunt, she must be extremely old.

"Have you met her yet?" he asked.

Sara looked at him, eyes bright with question.

"Alta? Not that she'd remember if you had. The old girl's 100, she'll be 101 come next March," Bob told her.

A hundred? Wow. Living in D.C., Sara barely ever saw anyone over retirement age, let alone someone close to a hundred. "Not yet," she said. "Has she lived here her entire life?"

"Yup, lived here her whole life, was born here. Her father built it," Bob said with a slight chuckle. He gestured toward the garden. "Alta planted this garden in her younger years and kept it goin'. She never left. Daddy didn't want any of his chicks strayin' too far from home. Abigail and William, her sister and brother, left the house, but stayed here in Middleburg."

"She never married?"

"Alta? No," Bob said. "Oh, she held a job – was a teacher for years. Had lots of suitors, too, but I reckon none of 'em could give her the sort of security her daddy could. So, she stayed." Bob tilted back his hat and wiped a bit of sweat from his brow. "Her daddy loved this place. Used to tell the kids lots of stories. He could remember when Indians camped right over there," he said pointing a finger toward the backyard. "Yup. Still find Confederate garb and arrow heads 'round here."

Sara looked around the yard, then up at the house. For an instant she thought she saw someone peering at her from a window. She closed her eyes. Opened them. Looked again. No one.

"I – I noticed a Confederate flag on my drive in," she said, moving deeper into the shade. Away from the gaze of the eye-like windows.

"Still some here, I suppose, who wish the South had won," Bob said with a shrug. He led Sara up the porch and gave a half knock on the screen door. "Martha!" he called, opening the door. "Martha stays with Alta 'til dark."

"She stays here alone at night?"

"She wouldn't have it any other way. Says she's perfectly safe in the house. Just likes Martha to help her out in the wakeful hours," he said and led her into the kitchen. "She's got the phone by the bed if she needs us," he said, nodding toward the adjacent room where a medical bed was set up.

The old woman sat in a chair near the bed. Her hair was white, not even a hint of color remained. She didn't seem to notice Bob or Sara. She held a newspaper close to her face, her glasses propped on her nose. The TV hummed quietly beneath the rustling of her turning pages, and the *thump, thump, thump* of her rocking chair that bumped softly against the wooden floor.

"Hello, Mr. Bob," came a sweet voice with a Hispanic accent.

"Martha," Bob nodded. "This is Sara Talbot. She's come all the way from D.C. to appraise the items in the house. Help her if she needs anything?"

Martha gave a curt nod. Her smile faded, eyes glided to the floor.

Bob handed Sara a piece of paper with a phone number on it. "Got things to do. Call me if you need anything."

"Will do," Sara said, placing the number in her pocket.

"Miss Altair, this lady is here to look at your house," Martha said.

Alta kept reading the paper, rocking, murmuring to herself. *Maybe this won't be too bad*, Sara thought. *Not if the old woman doesn't know what's happening.*

Martha motioned for Sara to follow her into Alta's living area, which appeared to be the only remodeled portion of the old home.

"She doesn't talk much. Mumbles sometimes. She'll go on about the paper, but not much else. Probably won't ever remember you were here," said Martha.

Sara looked around the room. Two old, sepia tone photos hung by Alta's bed. "Who are they?" she asked.

"They're Miss Altair's parents," said Martha. "Her father built the house. They both died here. Not in this room, died in the old bedroom," she said inclining her head toward the main house. "It's the sitting room now, but Miss Alta doesn't go into any other part of the house much anymore. Stays in here mostly. I fix her meals. Get here in the morning, leave around sunset." She shrugged. "I guess she sleeps most of the night. Seems to feel safe enough." She shivered. "I wouldn't want to stay here alone. At night. Especially not at night." Martha crossed herself.

Sara glanced at the housekeeper's serious brown eyes, at the cross dangling around her neck, and wondered why she'd said that. But Martha didn't speak further about it. She picked up a rag and began dusting.

Alta murmured something. She rocked slightly harder. Rustled the pages of her paper. *Thump, thump, thump.* The rocking chair banged against the floor in time with her whispers.

"What's she saying?"

"Something about 'the family'," Martha replied. "The past few days she started saying it. Keeps repeating something and then 'the family'. 'The family'. I don't know," Martha said with a frown. "Show you the house?"

Sara looked once more at the photos, then followed Martha through the kitchen and into a large pantry.

The pantry was well-stocked with jars of green beans, corn, beets, sweet potatoes, okra, peaches, and a variety of canned soups along with common sundries one would expect of a southern pantry.

"Who cans?" she asked.

"Her family," said Martha. "And I do some. It seems to make her happy when I do, especially when I use vegetables from her garden. She used to do it when she was younger they tell me. Made the best peach jam in town."

Sara's attention was caught by a bird that stared at her from its perch. It had been well preserved by some taxidermist long ago, but was now sitting in a lonely spot in the pantry. Its dark feathers were coated in dust, and it gazed intently at her with black, beady eyes. Eyes that seemed to follow her wherever she went.

"He bothered me, too," said Martha, grimacing at the bird. "Used to sit on Mr. Ward's desk there." She pointed to a desk and chair in the adjacent den. "I didn't like him staring at me all the time, so I moved him in here."

Sara didn't blame her for wanting that bird out of plain sight. There was something preternatural about its eyes. Something unearthly. Something haunted. She didn't like it.

"You like the desk?" Martha asked, leading them into the den and closing the pantry doors behind them. "It used to be in Mr. Ward's law office," she said, taking a rag from her apron pocket and gently wiping away a thin layer of dust from the desk's dark gain.

"Mr. Ward?"

"Miss Altair's father. He had a law office here in Middleburg. They told me that President Lincoln once sat in that chair when he was passing through."

"Really?"

"They have the papers, a book President Lincoln signed at the office, if you'd like to see them."

"I would. Thank you," she said.

"I'll have to look for them, but I may have to send copies to your office. May need Mr. Bob to find them," Martha said, opening the door from the den, and leading Sara into a large sitting room.

The room was musty. Blue carpet with a pink floral pattern covered the entire floor. It was worn in parts, moth-eaten. By the looks of it, it had been at least fifty years since the house had seen new carpet.

"This used to be the bedroom. Miss Altair was born in here."

Sara took note of a curio cabinet to her right filled with antique porcelain dishes and fine glassware. "This is where her parents died," Martha said, pointing past the cabinet to a corner of the room.

The faint outline of a headboard was barely visible against the wall. An uneasy feeling prickled along Sara's arms, down her spine.

A horrible moan pierced the stagnant silence.

"What was that?" Sara gasped.

"Miss Altair," said Martha, scurrying to the next room, the creaking pantry door slamming shut behind her.

"Well, I'd better get to work," Sara murmured to herself. She took a few tentative steps towards the room's center and sat on an old chaise lounge. She pulled out her notebook. Looked at the dusty porcelain, noting the fine late 19th century pieces, their floral patterns still crisp.

Her hand busily scrawled over the page when a cool breeze began to caress her face, like icy fingers against her skin. She dropped her notebook. Pulled back. Away from the disquieting touch.

She scanned the room, searching for the source of the breeze. The doors were closed, as were the windows. There was no air conditioner, no vents.

She listened.

The lonely ticking of a grandfather clock down the hall was all that kept her company. Then, beneath the layers of sound and silence, she could barely make out a faint moan. Alta's window unit in the room beyond, and then the almost inaudible murmur of Martha's voice.

Sweat trickled down the side of her face, her hair damp. An icy, invisible hand moved down her face, down her neck, leaving a trail of goose bumps in its wake.

She tried to call out, but her throat was dry with dusty fear. She couldn't move. Couldn't speak. Couldn't scream.

The hand caressed her shoulder. "Go away!" she whispered hoarsely, eyes wide with fear.

"Sorry?" asked Martha, the pantry door swinging closed behind her. "I came back as soon as I could. Miss Altair needed to get back to bed," she said, and then took a tentative step toward Sara. "You okay, Miss?"

Sara nodded, feeling as though she'd just been shaken awake from a dream. She took a deep breath and tried to rid herself of the uneasy feeling tickling the pit of her stomach.

"Why don't you show me the whole house, and then I'll take it room by room," she said, scooping up her notepad from the floor and attempting to regain her professional demeanor.

Martha looked skeptical, but opened a door on her right.

Through the doorway lay a darkened dining room. A round table of cherry wood was in the room's center, and three curio cabinets holding fine china lined the walls.

Sara took a step forward. Then another. Something stopped her. Her feet were like lead. Something or someone was in there. A presence larger than the room barred her entry. *It* was angry. She was not welcome.

"I'll go in there – later," she said almost inaudibly.

Martha nodded, seeming not to notice anything unusual, and proceeded towards the dark entryway that led to the winding, wooden stairway. She stopped at the foot of the stairs and beckoned past the rarely used front door. "That's the parlor, but Miss Altair might want to show it to you later herself."

"Show it to me? Herself?" Sara said, hearing her own hollow voice echo through the dim hallway. Her mind felt numb, foggy, as if the unseen presence was surrounding her again.

"If she's up to it. She still enjoys the parlor," Martha said, nodding toward the staircase. "The bedrooms are upstairs. The children used to sleep up there. When they were young. Miss Altair, her sister and brother."

A loud knock at the backdoor disturbed the silence. Sara lurched backward, bumping into the wall.

Martha gave her a sideways glance. "I need to get that," she said. "You can go up if you'd like. No one's up there. Just call if you need me."

Sara looked up the stairs. "I'll call if I need anything," she said with a weak smile.

Martha frowned, but disappeared back through the old bedroom to answer the door.

Sara was alone.

She took a deep, dust-filled breath. Her heart lurched against her stomach, pounded against her ribs. What would she find up there?

Don't be ridiculous. You've been in more than one "haunted house" and there's never been a problem. This is your business, she told herself. *An angry ghost or old woman won't stop you from assessing the property, for heaven's sake.* Forcing a false sense of calm upon herself, she placed her right foot tentatively on the first step.

Through the dim light she saw the same moth-eaten carpet covering the stairs. She exhaled, putting her full weight onto the second step. Not even the worn carpet padding could buffer the creaking old floor.

See, just the stairs creaking. Old wood. Nothing else.

She set one foot in front of the other, slowly carrying herself up the groaning, winding staircase. She counted. One step. Two. Three. . .

She kept her eyes forward. With every step, the dust danced in disturbed swirls, lit by slivers of sunlight that crept through cracks in the boarded windows.

She reached the top of the stairs, only twenty-seven of them, including the top landing. She peered over the railing at the lifeless chandelier hanging over the black abyss of the entry below. Its crystals, like cataracts, were so clouded with age and dust that she couldn't even detect the slightest sparkle of their former beauty.

Her feet cautiously made their way to the upstairs hall. The door to her left was slightly ajar. Sara slid her hand over the white door, across a tarnished nameplate: Altair.

The door opened silently. She reached into the room, flicked on a light switch. The lights still worked. They weren't stark or overly bright, but she could see well enough. The bedroom was musty. Particles of dust rose in the air; no cleaner's hand had been here in decades.

Ahead was a four-poster bed of dark cherry wood, its lacy coverlet under a fine film of dust. To the left of the bed was a nightstand with a pink Tiffany lamp and several framed pictures. She could tell that one of the young women was Alta; perhaps the others were family.

She carefully opened the nightstand drawer. Several yellowing black and white photographs, along with a few sepia tones, were bundled together. Sara removed the one from the top. A picture of a stern looking man gazed back at her. She flipped the picture over. Written on the back of the photo was *father, 1898.*

The next picture was that of three children. Sara could just make out Alta standing between the other two. She must have been no more than five. A pretty girl. The other children, both slightly older than Alta, must have been her brother and sister. Scrawled writing on the back of the photograph confirmed Sara's guess: William, Altair, Abigail.

She put the photos back in their place. Looked around. Dusty, white lace curtains hung in the shuttered window to her left, next to which set an oak vanity and matching chair. The mirror above the vanity was crinkled and dark with age, offering only ghostly reflections of the room.

Sara felt drawn by the decrepit looking glass. She sat on the faded crimson velvet of the vanity seat and gazed at herself in the crackled mirror, warped and twisted by age. She stared at her contorted image, beyond herself. Beyond the mirror. Beyond the room.

A cool giggle embraced her. A child's laughter. The sound crept under her skin like a crisp breeze, sending a cold shiver of fear rippling along her flesh. Her breath grew heavy and rapid and shown in the air, but still she gazed more deeply.

A soft exhalation tickled hairs on the back of her neck. She could see nothing but her own dilated pupils gazing back at her.

She waited. Tried to hold back her breath. Tried to look into the mirror, into the room. Someone else was beside her. Breathing. Looking down on her. Her eyes skimmed across the surface of the mirror. No one.

Terror seeped through her pours like poison immobilizing its prey. She could not escape lest she turned to look. Her heart thumped in her throat, constricting her airway.

Again, the giggle.

Through the mirror's reflection she saw a little girl standing behind her. Pale, wispy, ghostly. She looked exactly like the older girl in the photograph. Alta's sister. Abigail.

Sara closed her eyes, squeezed them tight. She wanted to wake up, wanted to run away, wanted to scream. She wanted to call out to Martha, but no sound escaped her lips. Her mind filled with mist, her head light. She opened her eyes.

The little girl was gone. But under the covers of the dusty bed lay the shape of a man. His chest rising and falling in ragged breaths.

She forced herself to stand, her legs like heavy crystal. She wanted to break free, to run. But, something held her to the spot. She saw her hand reaching out in front of her. She tried to stop it. Couldn't.

Her fingers clasped around the white coverlet. The cold breath of the mummy-like form caressed her fingers. Her mind commanded her to stop. To run. To scream. But her hand moved without thought.

She threw the coverlet back, and let out an ear-piercing scream.

A translucent man lay before her. The man from the photograph. Alta's father. He stared straight at her. His brown eyes glistened in the dim light, his mouth gaped open to speak.

His hatred roiled around her, twisting the air to his will. His hatred for all who tried to dismantle his home, for all who tried destroy his nest. Hands outstretched, he rose to take hold of her.

She cried out, panic catching in her throat. She tried to run, but couldn't move.

The little girl giggled, and a cold, small hand pulled her back to the vanity.

She looked at Sara and smiled. "We're supposed to keep it in the family," she said, and then turned back to the mirror. Her reflection was no longer that of a little girl, but the aging effigy of Abigail.

Sara's screams gave way to movement. She ran away from the man, away from bedroom, away from the awful giggles.

She stopped in the darkness of the silent hallway, panting to catch her breath. She peered into a shadowy, empty doorway that led to a boarded up balcony. No way out except to go back, past the room. Past the girl. Past *him*.

She turned towards the stairs. Stopped. A wispy ball of light floated along the hallway enticing her forward. It glided along until it disappeared into one of the rooms.

It was like a beacon. A hypnotic light. She had to follow. Down the hall, along the moth-eaten carpet, and around the banister to the darkened room where the light had disappeared.

The door of the room was ajar, only a pale, ethereal light emanated from the darkness. Upon the door was a brass plate inscribed with a name: William.

The crackling sound of a gramophone began to hiss softly, along with a muffled, indistinguishable thumping. Heaviness filled her stomach, her arms, her legs. A sense of dread engulfed her. It was as if the music called her – as if *he* willed her to him.

Her heart hammered an eerie rhythm against her ribs. She was no longer in control of her own legs, her own will. One step, and another and another. She moved towards the door.

The stairs, her only escape, lay behind her.

A fetid smell emanated from somewhere within the room. She couldn't breathe. Couldn't move. Couldn't speak. The lights flickered and a sense of despair and fear and hatred filled her. It pressed down on her, crushing her.

Help me! Must run! Must scream! Help me!

Her lips didn't move, only her eyes. Frantically searching for a way out.

The door slowly opened. A young man, ghostly, ethereal, sat in a rocking chair. Staring at her.

Thump. Thump. Thump.

The chair kept rocking, and he kept staring. Staring at her. Staring with sad, longing eyes. William.

Then she felt the malicious presence again . . . *he* was behind her.

The putrid smell grew almost unbearable, like the rotting flesh of a rodent trapped within the wall of a house. Her eyes filled with tears. But still she could not utter a sound, could not run away. She felt herself falling into darkness, slipping into some black chasm where *he* waited for her.

The sad man rose from the rocking chair, tossed the gramophone to the floor. "*Run away! Go now,*" he urged her. "*Go now, while you can.*" His lips didn't move, but his words rang in her ears.

Like a noose, *his* grip tightened around her. Her vision narrowed into a ribbon of blackness. The young man screamed. "*Father, no!*"

With a sudden thrust to her chest, Sara was thrown backward into the hallway. Away from the room. Away from the man. Away from the mist that fogged her mind. The door slammed shut, and the house shook.

It was all the distraction she needed.

Thank you, William. Thank you!

From behind the closed door she could still hear William's urging: "*Go, now. Run away. Run. Leave this place. We will keep it. Run!*"

She raced down the stairs. *His* laughter rumbled through the house. The curio cabinets shook. The walls shook. The floors shook. But she kept running.

She slammed open the doors into the parlor. Her mind raced; her stomach churned with sickness. She could still hear William urging her away. *His* laughter echoing through the halls.

She threw the door open and ran into Alta's living quarters.

Alta stood, swaying on her partially crippled legs. She clawed at Sara's arm with yellowing nails. Sara pulled, tried to get free, but the old woman's grip was fierce.

The old woman cackled, her voice growing deeper and deeper. She looked at Sara, her eyes glazed over in an opaque film. Sara screamed and tore herself from Alta's talon-like fingers, leaving jagged, bloody rips in her skin.

The pain didn't matter. She had to run, to escape. She could see the door, the light outside.

She heard Alta's voice, "Daddy always said to keep it in the family." Her old woman tones contorted into that of an angry, powerful man. "Keep it in the family! Keep it in the family!"

The coarse cackling began again, pitching from that of the old woman to that of her father.

Sara didn't look back.

Outside air embraced her, fresh against her skin. The screen door slammed shut behind her and she fell from the porch, skinning her knee on the crushed limestone path. A cloud of dust rose, filling her mouth and nostrils.

She coughed, struggled to stand. A little hand touched her. She shrieked. Pulled back in fear, but the hand was still there. Warm and soft and gentle.

A little boy. A little, alive boy, met her eyes. He looked startlingly like William.

Sara shuddered.

"You've seen *him*, haven't you?" he asked.

Sara nodded numbly.

"I told Uncle Bob not to have people come, strangers. Strangers like you. *He* won't let it be sold. None of it," the boy said. "I've seen *him*, too. I'm his great-great-great nephew. Somethin' like that. I'll inherit this place when Aunt Alta dies," he said with a shrug of resignation. "Uncle Bob doesn't want it, but we don't have a choice. We have to keep it in the family."

Shadows in Georgetown

Donald Jeffries

Anna was a nervous child. She was unduly afraid of a good many things, but she especially feared death.

She came by this naturally; her peculiar family was obsessed with the dead and the dying. Her mother and grandmother talked about it constantly. Despite all her efforts at resistance, Anna was morbidly drawn to the subject, too. She spent many nights trembling under the covers, trying to forget the tales discussed at the dinner table, regarding sudden heart attacks, fatal falls and tragic drowning.

Anna's family members often referenced the "shadows" that haunted Georgetown, the section of Washington, D.C. where they resided. They intimated that these shadows were everywhere, and the idea terrified nine year old Anna.

"Watch out," Anna's haggard Grandmother would constantly warn her whenever she left the house, "Don't let the shadows get you."

Anna was also intrigued by ghosts. She gobbled up every book that touched on them in the Georgetown public library. In fact, anything with dark or sinister overtones interested her. Bram Stoker's *Dracula* was her favorite novel. The writing was too sophisticated for many much older than her, but nine year old Anna understood every word.

The year was 1920 and Washington, D.C. was in a state of transition. No longer the flea-infested swamp land it had been for most of the nineteenth century, signs of a thriving modern metropolis were springing up everywhere. Anna was a child of the times; she'd been walking or riding her bike by herself, all over Washington, D.C., for a few years already. She'd frequently go as far as the National Zoo, contentedly gazing at the elephants and hippos with no one accompanying her. She wasn't the only youngster left alone and unprotected in those days.

Anna's zeal for adventure was always tempered by the things she heard every day in her weird household. The shadows, especially, kept creeping into her mind; she often imagined they were behind her, peering over her shoulders. Every time, in fact, she saw her own shadow, she shuddered in fear. Still, she couldn't help but observe it closely. More importantly, she couldn't stop herself from wondering where those *other* shadows were.

Anna had a younger brother, but her older sister had died when she was only three years old. Anna had heard the story so many times, recounted by various female relatives with an unnatural amount of gusto and glee. Little Nancy had simply dropped dead one sunny afternoon. That, of course, would be rare enough for a toddler, but it was the circumstances under which it happened that really gave it such an odd distinction.

Anna was an infant at the time, and had been left home in the care of her father. Her mother, grandmother and two aunts had gone to Mount Olivet Cemetery, which was predictably enough a favorite picnic spot of theirs. Nearly every Sunday, they would lay flowers in front of the tombstones of Anna's maternal great-grandparents, spread a blanket over the area and then enjoy their lunch. Usually, they would leave Nancy at home with her father, too, but this time they took her. They would come to rue that decision.

While they were munching on fried chicken and engaging in wicked gossip, Nancy, allowed to roam free around the adjacent gravesites, wandered off towards some thick woods which bordered the eastern corner of Mount Olivet. One of her aunts belatedly noticed this, and raced after the three year old, who was merely a speck in the distance by this time. What Aunt Isabelle would claim to see as she approached the woods would later be debated and disputed by members of the family.

"There was a dark figure, half hiding," Isabelle would invariably say, "kind of gray, with the brightest red eyes you ever saw. There was a mist all around it, and a horrible smell."

By the time Isabelle, with the others close behind her, arrived at the spot, the mysterious figure was nowhere to be seen. Nancy's tiny, lifeless body was lying in a brown circle where the grass had been burned away. Nancy's mother gathered up her baby and wept profusely over her, but like many a bereaved parent before and after her, found that tears could not revive her. Autopsies, especially for children, weren't performed very often in those days, but Nancy's family demanded one. Unfortunately, the doctors couldn't determine what caused her death. Nothing *natural* kills a three year old, and there had been no accident.

Anna's family would speculate about it ever afterwards, but they would never be able to reconcile themselves with what was a truly unexplainable event. They simply attributed it to the shadows, and came to believe more firmly than ever in their ubiquitous presence.

While they would discuss Nancy's demise constantly, the family never went back to Mount Olivet Cemetery again. Thus, Anna had never been there. Nearly every day, she would ride her bike past the wrought iron entrance gates, slowing down to take in the scenery. She wanted desperately to go inside those gates, and to venture out past her great-grandparents' graves, to the very spot where *it* happened. This wouldn't give her any answers, of course, but she needed to see the spot where her sister's young life had so inexplicably ended.

Anna could see the cemetery's office from the sidewalk. She was a very intelligent girl, and had already planned to ask them where her great grandparents were buried. From there, she would simply look for the woods. Legend had it that the spot where Nancy's body had been found had never grown grass since, so Anna reasoned it should be easy to locate.

While Anna was inordinately interested in the details about Nancy's death, and possessed a tremendously inquisitive nature in general, her slew of powerful fears kept her from actually doing anything. She'd sigh deeply, then peddle past the cemetery, and wind up at the Smithsonian museum or the zoo. Maybe if she'd had an adventurous friend, it might have been different. She needed someone to push her.

Finally, one unnaturally cold spring day, she summoned up the courage. It was totally spontaneous; she'd stopped her bike momentarily, as she often did, and an instant after starting to peddle away, she suddenly veered left and was through the entrance gates before she realized it. Once she was inside, Anna kept going and got the information she needed from the person who worked in the cemetery office. Her great-grandparents were buried at the far end of Mount Olivet, so Anna had to pass by most of the graves along the way. She tried not to read too many of the tombstones, but the lure was irresistible.

The ones who'd died at young ages really fascinated her, which was probably natural for a nine year old. *All those names,* she mused to herself, *breathing and playing just like me and now they're mostly bones and dust.* It was a jarring thought for such an innocent mind. There were elaborate, ornate stones everywhere, with a handful of truly spectacular memorials to lost loved ones. At length, Anna arrived at the place where her great grandparents were buried. They'd died before she was born, but Anna paid a proper moment's respect on her knees, and leaving her bike laying between graves, slowly sauntered towards the woods, which loomed in the distance to the east.

When she came within a few paces of the woods, it didn't take her long to find *the* spot. The circle was large enough to stand out prominently, and its dull, brownish color was in stark contrast to the manicured grass bordering it. There was a strange stillness in the air now, and it seemed to calm Anna, who should have been very, very afraid at this point. Abandoning all her customary fears, the little girl gingerly placed her right foot inside the grassless circle.

Suddenly Anna heard a deep voice coming from her right.

"You won't find your sister here," a gruesome looking dark spectre stepped out from behind an imposing old elm tree. "And you'll never solve *that* mystery, no matter how hard you try."

He threw a half vaporous head back, exposing in full his jet black goatee, and laughed manically. He then approached Anna, who was powerless to run away. The figure appeared more to be floating than walking. The grey phantom placed his hand, which was unbearably warm, on Anna's shoulder and gazed deeply into her eyes. The youngster felt paralyzed as the monstrous apparition planted a lengthy and painful kiss on her forehead. His foul, ugly lips left a blasphemous mark there, accompanied by an uncomfortable stinging sensation. Anna closed her eyes, to avoid seeing that hideous face, and when she opened them he was gone. Able to move at last, Anna ran off without a single look behind her.

All at once, it began to rain incredibly hard. Sheets of water bounced off the tombstones with a macabre rhythm. Anna slipped on the suddenly wet ground and landed head first next to an open, gaping grave. As she raised her eyes toward the freshly sculpted tombstone, she gasped aloud. *Her* name was carved there, with the present day's date chiseled right after the "D."

The terrified little girl scrambled to her feet and continued on through the graveyard, which seemed somehow a lot larger now. Eventually she passed her great-grandparents' plots, and nearly fainted when she saw the ground begin to move, and a couple of ghoulish green, twisted fingers emerge through the earth there.

Anna couldn't find her bike anywhere, so she ran as fast as she could, with the rain beating down incessantly, and at long last she rushed through the entrance gates, moments before they inexplicably clanged shut behind her. Breathing a huge sigh of relief, Anna realized that the massive outpouring of rain had ceased as abruptly as it had started.

The little girl was stunned and dumbfounded. She stumbled through the cobbled streets of the city, and it was quite a while before she began to realize that most of the people she passed were staring at her. She felt their eyes, which were seemingly all concentrated on her forehead. Many of them whispered in audible tones, *"She's got the mark, alright"* and *"Don't touch her!"*

Finally, Anna stopped to catch her breath. She rested her body against the plate glass window of a five and dime store, and turned around to check her reflection out. There was a dark, noticeable mark squarely in the middle of her forehead. Anna didn't recognize the distinct symbol, but it looked inherently evil to her. It was as if she'd been branded. She couldn't bear to see it and turned away in disgust. As she did so, she found herself facing an imposing figure in blue.

"Alright, little miss," the huge police officer with the unfriendly, ruddy face bent down so that she could all too clearly see his dishonest yellowed eyes. "Come along now. We have some questions for you."

The policeman grabbed her firmly by the arm and practically carried her to the Metropolitan Police station. As they walked past the front desk, a few other officers smiled knowingly and winked at her. A middle aged secretary emerged from an office, pointed in horror at Anna, covered her mouth and dashed into the rest room.

Anna was whisked into an interrogation room, where a thin detective with a dark, wrinkled face was chain smoking cigarettes. The little girl was shoved into a wooden chair and the detective slid his own chair right next to hers.

"Well," the detective blew his cigarette smoke directly into Anna's face, "W*hat* did you see? *What* do you know?" He grabbed the shivering youngster by her shoulders.

Anna couldn't speak. She had no idea why this was happening. She felt like she was having the worst nightmare of her young life.

The detective threw down his cigarette and stamped it out on the floor, less than an inch from Anna's foot. "Tell us everything!" He screamed into her ears.

Anna's parents would discover her bike, lying behind some bushes just inside the entrance to Mount Olivet Cemetery. They notified the police, but the authorities were unable to give them any answers. Nine year old Anna was never seen again. The family became even more preoccupied with death and the darker aspects of our existence, having lost two children to the shadows lurking everywhere in the city.

Tracks

Scott Woodward

"Thomas?" Jason recoiled from the apparition standing in the doorway of a townhouse with a cracked porch light and mud-streaked entryway.

Thomas managed a smile and motioned him inside. Jason hesitated, wondering just how far down the ladder of despair his friend had descended, and then followed him into the dim interior.

"It's good to see you," Thomas said climbing onto a wooden bar stool at the kitchen island. His feet were wrapped in layers of filthy, bloodstained rags giving them the appearance of misshapen hooves. He stared at Jason for a moment and an expression scuttled across his face, but was gone before Jason could identify it.

For the second time in as many minutes Jason wondered if he had made a mistake in coming. He hadn't seen Thomas since they served together at the Embassy in Caracas and he hardly looked like the same person.

"Do you remember the tracks?" Thomas asked, running a raw-knuckled hand through a mop of disheveled, graying hair.

How could he forget? They had appeared after the first snowfall of the season and had been found scattered across Loudoun County. Grotesque prints that suggested their maker had feet with three clawed toes in front and two in the back of its foot where a heel should have been. They were widely assumed to be a hoax.

The so-called "cannibal murders" had begun shortly after the first tracks were reported.

"Yes, I remember," Jason answered. "Some were found not too far from here, right?"

Thomas paused for a moment. "Closer than you might think," he said, nodding toward the back yard.

Jason turned and stared out the window, but saw only a deepening gloom as night enveloped the townhouse.

"They weren't a hoax," Thomas said after several minutes. "I know. I put my foot in one." He shuddered and stared at Jason. "Lara saw them also," he added referring to his on-again, off-again girlfriend.

"What did they look like?"

"Same as they described in *The Informer* only larger and the two toes in the back, where a heel should have been, they faced backwards."

"What do you think made them?" Jason felt the skin of his neck tighten.

"I don't know; maybe the Wendigo."

Jason cocked his head. What in God's name was a wendigo? Thomas said it as if naming some well-known animal common to Northern Virginia.

"Whatever made them," Thomas continued, "it stood right there on our deck and watched us through the window."

"Jesus."

"That's not the worst part," Thomas said, his lips trembling. "After I stepped in the tracks…" he trailed off and swallowed several times before continuing. "Ever since then, things have changed. I've changed." Thomas buried his face in his hands.

He might have been sobbing, but for some reason Jason thought he was laughing.

Gayle unlocked the door to her townhouse and raced a gust of arctic wind inside. She flipped on the foyer light and shrugged off her wool coat. She realized she must have forgotten to turn up the thermostat, as it felt almost as cold inside her townhouse as outside.

The evening had been disheartening. Dropping off her two sons at what used to be her house, she had seen Natalie, who had been her neighbor, carrying boxes inside. It was the indignity of being summarily replaced that was the worst of it.

She half suspected Dave had arranged the timing to ensure she had seen Natalie traipsing between houses. She wouldn't have been completely surprised if Natalie had been naked. Dave had probably even asked.

She shook her head. The bastard; people never wanted what they had.

A draft, seeping from underneath the basement door, reminded her that she was still standing in the foyer staring absently into the coat closet. She frowned and slammed the closet door shut with more force than she had intended.

Another door slammed shut upstairs.

Gayle froze, considering the possibilities. The sound of footsteps bounding across the master bedroom toward the stairs spurred her to action.

She whirled toward the front door, teeth clenched. No matter who the intruder was, there was no way he could get down the stairs before she could reach the front door.

The intruder didn't bother with the stairs. It tore through the master bedroom doorway, hurdled the banister, and crashed to the wood floor nine feet below.

Gayle had just grabbed the door knob when she felt a hand grasp her ponytail and savagely yank her head backwards. Her neighbor, Lara, leered down at her.

"I partake of this communion with the Great Wendigo," Lara whispered as she thrust a clawed finger into Gayle's eye socket.

"Do you want to see them?"

"Won't they be buried?" Jason asked, motioning out the window to the snow that was now descending in sheets beyond the pale glow of the porch light.

"Perhaps," Thomas said. "But they'll still be there."

"Okay," Jason said with more enthusiasm than he felt.

Jason pulled on his damp coat and glanced around the disarrayed interior of the house as he followed Thomas to the door leading to the deck. A numbing blast of air shrieked through the cracked door and gouged his face.

"Ready?" Thomas asked, looking back, a gloved hand fighting the wind for control of the door.

Jason nodded and tucked his chin against his chest as he followed Thomas onto the deck, which was covered with at least a foot of snow. Neither spoke as they trudged across the deck.

Thomas stopped in front of a window and squatted, clearing the freshly-fallen snow with a gloved hand. Jason stood above him, leaning forward as he watched Thomas, using both hands now, continue to paw through the layers of new snow.

A layer of frozen snow was slowly uncovered and Thomas's gloved hands increased their tempo. Clearing more snow away, Jason could see the outlines of a grotesque track frozen in the crusted snow.

The exposed track was at least two feet in length and nearly a foot wide. Jason could see where claws from each of the three front toes had sunk into the pine wood. The claws from the two rear-facing toes had similarly marred the deck.

"Jesus," he whispered, squatting to trace the outline of the print with a gloved finger.

"Help me uncover the rest," Thomas said.

Hours later, they could see that the tracks crisscrossed the entire surface of the deck in an almost spiral pattern. Thomas began to pace alongside the tracks, as if accompanying whatever had made them.

Jason lit a cigarette and then walked to the nearest corner of the deck, several feet from the patio door, where he noticed several other prints nearby. Looking closer he could see two sets of boot prints, a larger and a smaller one.

The snow was churned up in places, and it looked as if the person wearing the larger boots had dragged the smaller person across the deck. After a space, the smaller set of prints disappeared entirely, only to reappear inside the grotesque tracks. Jason stared for a moment, trying to interpret the scene.

"She was frightened," Thomas said, right behind him.

Jason whirled to face him. He hadn't even heard him approach. Thomas smiled with teeth filed to jagged points.

"But she's no longer frightened," he whispered, more to himself than to Jason, looking at the cloudy sky. "Everything changes after you walk in *his* tracks. The craving drives out everything else."

"What are you talking about?" Jason took a step back.

Thomas's head snapped down like a snake's and his eyes gleamed in the faint porch light.

"I know about you and Lara," he said, and lunged forward. "Not that it matters now."

Sometime later Jason made it back to his condo in Ashburn. He had seen only a few other vehicles driving erratically on the slushy roads. He turned onto Ashburn Village Road, and saw more of the tracks. A group of small children dressed in brightly colored coats had been gathered around the prints.

His right elbow was swollen and ached where he had slammed it into Thomas's head, and blood was seeping through the tear on the left side of his jacket. When Thomas had lunged forward he had pivoted and struck him in the head with his elbow. This had saved his life, as Thomas's jaws had torn into his shoulder rather than his throat.

They had scuffled and Jason had managed to escape, but not before his left foot had sunk into one of the tracks. It had only been one foot, but that might have been enough.

A gust of wind rattled the condo's sliding glass door like an ethereal claw pulling at the handle. It had been like this ever since his foot had plunged into that track, a sense of being stalked.

He rubbed his eyes and stared out the window, away from the blue glow of his laptop's screen. He had been searching for anything he could find about the Wendigo Thomas had mentioned, and had been surprised by the amount of information available on the Internet.

While much of the information was fragmentary and contradictory, a prevalent theme was that the Wendigo was some kind of malevolent winter spirit from Native American lore and figured prominently in the beliefs of Virginia tribes, especially the Powhatan. According to legend, the Wendigo could possess a victim, causing that person to become a cannibal. Most of the scholars agreed the legend was designed to reinforce taboos against cannibalism, especially during severe famines, such as the Virginia Harrowing of 1778. None of the articles suggested how an individual became possessed.

Jason cracked his knuckles and leaned against the wooden back of his chair. None of this made any sense.

He got up, grabbed a pack of cigarettes off the kitchen island, and wandered out onto the second floor deck. The illumination from the porch light seemed muted, as if suffocated by the cold. It had grown so cold outside that it looked as if even the sky had frozen.

A single blow might shatter it entirely, revealing the realm of the Great Wendigo.

Jason shook his head. The thought seemed to have originated from outside his consciousness, as if he were now attuned to some alien frequency and receiving transmissions from an unknown sender.

A tremendous wave of displaced air crashed over his apartment building and Jason felt the wooden balcony lurch downward under its weight. He grabbed the railing with both hands and searched the night skyline for the cause of the windstorm.

Overhead he could hear something monstrous striding through the frigid sky. A colossal shadow, darker than the cloud-streaked sky, loomed over the building and Jason shrank back into a corner of the balcony. The temperature plummeted as the shadow passed directly overhead. The deck light flared and then burst.

Jason remained slumped in a corner trembling until the shadow receded into the distance and he could no longer hear the friction of vast strides through the atmosphere. He rose on shaky legs to witness a pack of feral suburbanites loping along the ground beneath his balcony, trailing their new master. Many of them carried clubs, knives, or improvised weapons, and a few were covered in dark stains. For a brief moment Jason felt an impulse to vault the railing and join them.

A sliding glass door screeched open downstairs and Jason saw his voluble neighbor Joe emerge, dressed in a faded army surplus jacket thrown over plaid pajamas.

"Hey," Joe yelled. "What's the ruckus?"

The pack wheeled about and several of its faster members were on him in seconds. One raised a golf club and Jason heard a sound like a cantaloupe being split with a bat. Joe's body collapsed backward, crashing through the sliding glass door.

The entire pack, maybe twenty individuals, streamed into the apartment and out of Jason's view. The screams started moments later and Jason remembered that Joe had a long-suffering wife, Becky; a kind heart married to a lager lout. The screams devolved in hysterical whimpering and then eventually gurgled into silence.

After a few more minutes the pack filed out of apartment and disappeared into the night without a single glance back. Spattered stains and shredded clothing were visible among the trampled snow.

Jason crept inside and locked the sliding glass door behind him. Why hadn't anyone called the police? Why hadn't he?

Depeche Mode's *Blasphemous Rumors* filled his apartment and Jason lunged toward the kitchen island where he had left his cell phone.

"Hello," he said.

"Why are you whispering?" Lara asked.

"Jesus," he said. "Where are you?"

Something about that amused her and he could hear her chuckle softly. He also heard what sounded like gasping in the background.

"Are you all right?"

"*I'm* fine," she replied.

Cold fingers wormed through his intestines. He stared out the window as he cradled the cell phone in his hand and recalled an image of two small boot prints inside of a giant clawed track.

"Where are you?"

"At a friend's, where are *you*?" she asked.

Jason hesitated.

"I bet you're at home," Lara said, filling the silence. "Maybe I should pay you a visit."

Jason stiffened. "Maybe you should," he said. "I'll be here."

"I'm on my way." The line went dead.

Lara hung up and turned to look at Gayle, gagged and tied to her own bed. Several knives, gleaming in the candlelight,

110

lay strewn across the bed and strips of skin glistened on the wall like freckled wallpaper.

The wind shook the townhouse and Lara could sense the Great Wendigo's sanctifying presence. She thrust her left hand into her mouth and ground her teeth together, gulping down the severed digits and cascading blood.

Lara fell to her knees and threw back her head, vomiting a shriek laden with a millennium of malice and corpses. Outside, the wind rose and fell in an accompanying howl, and she sprang to her feet, heeding the Great Wendigo's call.

Grinning, she picked up a knife and loomed over Gayle, who shook her head violently back and forth in a silent plea. Lara's lips curled back in a lupine smile. She didn't have much time, but she had enough.

Jason slammed down the phone. His eyes darted around the room, looking for something to use as a weapon. Lara was on her way.

His eyes fixed on the computer screen and he rushed over to the laptop and typed a few words frantically into a search engine. Half reading and half listening for any sound at his door, or even the balcony, he searched for methods to kill someone possessed by the Wendigo.

It was less than an hour later when he heard a stealthy tread on the carpeted stairs outside his apartment door. He glanced at the pots of water sputtering on the stove and walked on the balls of his feet into the small family room that connected the foyer to the kitchen. Standing rigid he strained to identify any sound beyond his shallow breathing.

The footsteps receded down the stairwell and he heard the door to the apartment building bang shut.

He remained motionless. Had she really left the building or was she trying to trick him into opening the door? Holding his breath, he crept to the front door and peered through the peephole into an empty stairwell.

The rear sliding glass door exploded inward in a cloud of shards as a small figure hurtled into the apartment and landed in a crouch.

"Miss me?" Lara's eyes blazed. She shook her head, sending pieces of glass spewing from her hair.

"Lara?" She looked savage, almost primal, and was between him and the kitchen.

"It hasn't been that long." She smiled, revealing stained and jagged teeth. Jason backed slowly toward the front door.

On the stove one of the pots boiled over, sending a stream of hissing water cascading down the front of the oven and onto the linoleum floor.

Lara's head whipped to the left and Jason heard a low growl issue from her throat. She turned and glared at Jason. "Defiler!"

Jason gulped and prepared to flee out the apartment's front door. But Lara was faster. A hand, so cold it seared his flesh, closed around his forearm and yanked him forward.

"Pour that filth down the drain or I'll rip you apart...limb by limb."

Given the ease with which she had pulled him across the room, Jason had no doubt Lara possessed the strength to do it. The blood staining the front of her sweater suggested she might have done something similar to someone else.

She herded him into the kitchen and shoved him toward the stove, her right hand still clasped around his arm.

"Now," Lara tightened her grip and Jason winced as the bones in his arm grated together.

With his right arm he grabbed a pot of boiling water from the closest burner and turned to his left, as if to head toward the sink. At the last moment, he twisted and flung the pot's boiling contents onto Lara's face.

She screeched and staggered back, trying to grab his arm with her left hand. But that hand was missing three fingers and Jason was able to pull free of its grasp.

Still clutching his left arm in her right hand, Lara stretched her jaws wide and pulled Jason toward her face. Off balance, Jason grasped a second pot from the stove and arced it over his head, splashing its contents down Lara's throat.

The icy hand released its grip and Lara staggered backwards, her mangled hand clutching at her chest. She sank to her knees. Tears streamed down her face and her eyes rolled

112

backwards, revealing yellowed orbs. A thin wail wheezed from between her clenched teeth and she toppled forward to lay sprawled on the kitchen floor. A violent gust of wind shook the apartment.

Jason prodded the body with his foot and, when there was no movement, knelt beside his former lover. He wiped a tear from her cheek and whispered a remembered prayer from his childhood.

Rising, he saw displayed on the screen of his laptop the website, *Eldritch Lore*, with its banner reading "Reclaiming the Earth, One Abomination at a Time." Beneath that was guidance on destroying those possessed by the Great Wendigo. One had to melt their frozen hearts.

He staggered to the bathroom, undressed and turned the shower to just short of scalding. He wasn't sure what he would say to the police. Given what he had seen tonight, he suspected they would have their hands full and wouldn't overly scrutinize his story of a crazed intruder.

Twenty minutes later, skin steamed pink, he shut off the water and pulled the shower curtain open. He stepped onto the rug and planted his feet as he began to towel his body, trying to envision his life without Lara.

A numbing chill crept up his legs and he looked down to see both his feet embedded in tracks formed by the sopping, matted fiber of the rug. They were the monstrous three-toed tracks of the Wendigo.

Before the World Fell

Daniel Fobes

Hugh crouched, assault rifle gripped tight in sweaty hands, in what once was an upscale bookstore on the corner of I Street and 19th, about four blocks from the White House. Surrounding him were the skeletal remains of metal shelves, some toppled over, others still upright, though all devoid of books. What wasn't carried away during the initial looting had become fuel for fires over the past ten years.

He peered out onto the street, still choked with the rusted remains of automobiles; silent testimony to what once had been the capital of the richest country in the world. The August sun glared through the shattered glass storefront making the heat inside the building almost unbearable. Still, Hugh knew that it was suicide to change locations in the middle of the day. While the morning and the evening were relatively safe for travel, the day and the night were deadly. He looked on as a rail-thin dog poked among the ash and ruin looking for the smallest morsel of food. *Poor thing isn't going to last long out there* he mused.

As if in answer to the thought, a shadow swooped along the street, black, large and fast. It was only visible for a second, but it was a second longer than Hugh wished. Its hairy body resembled something between a bat, a gorilla and an octopus. Like an image from a nightmare, this horrendous creature, thick of body with tentacle-like appendages flew on large hairy wings. In between breaths, the dog was gone and the street revealed no further movement.

Hugh waited impatiently until the sun dipped low and the storefront fell into shadow. Slowly, painfully, he rose to a crouch, blood seeping back into his legs. With carefully placed steps, he moved to the recesses of the building, still watching the street for any signs of life.

Reaching the back of the store, Hugh turned and slid through an open doorway into the coolness of the back room. A storeroom that now stockpiled only dust and cobwebs was on one side; a closed door with a faded sign revealing it to be an office was on the other. Hugh stopped for a second. Closed doors were a rarity nowadays outside of human fortifications, and he was intrigued. The cool metal felt good in the palm of his hand as he slowly turned the doorknob. The door swung only a fraction of an inch, however, and then stopped.

Hugh pressed his weight against the door and sluggishly it began to give. Pulling a flashlight from his satchel, he opened the door enough to poke his head in, and shone the light into the room. In its feeble ray, he saw the remains of a desk and his nose was apprised of a not-unfamiliar smell, referred to among his peers as "old putrid." Sure enough, on the floor next to a couple of cardboard boxes were moldy human remains. Some poor soul had barricaded himself in the room and died alone of thirst, injury, or at his own hand. It wasn't Hugh's first find of this sort.

As he pushed open the door, Hugh glimpsed a book on the floor. It had a familiar aspect and he leaned in and used his flashlight to fish it to within reach. It was a hard-bound edition of *The Lord of the Rings* by JRR Tolkien. The funny thing about it was the errant scratch on the cover that exactly matched the scratch on the copy Jaena had bought when they first met over thirteen years ago.

Hugh paused, lost in the memory. He had first seen Jaena in a bookstore, not unlike the one he now stood in, and was instantly drawn to her—it wasn't every day he saw a beautiful woman holding one of his favorite books; a book that for him represented an entry to another world of fantasy and adventure. She was in the Classic Literature section with that book, scratch and all, in her hand when he approached her. He asked, "Do you realize that Tolkien is the father of everything that is awesome in the world?"

She raised her eyebrows skeptically. "And what's that supposed to mean?"

"I mean," Hugh explained, "Everything you've seen in movies, read in books or played in games that said that dwarves were short, hairy men with a penchant for ale, that elves were tall slender people with pointy ears, and orcs were mean, nasty brutes, all originated in that book."

115

Jaena laughed and said, "Cool—I would never have thought of it that way."

"I think that one is damaged," Hugh pointed at the defect on the cover, "I'm sure the store has more copies."

"No," she smiled after glancing down at the book, "I like it. It gives it character."

That was the beginning of a beautiful romance—one that was, he remembered painfully, cruelly interrupted by the Invasion.

Hugh stashed the book in his knapsack and began to move again. There were only a couple of hours till nightfall, and if there was any place he did not want to be, it was out and about after sunset. Rifle at the ready, he moved to the back exit of the bookstore.

The rear of the store opened to a long dark hall that crossed the width of a city block. Back in the day, it had been the pedestrian walkway for a mall. Tracks in the decade's accumulation of dust testified to the importance that the passage had for the surviving humans. Hugh followed the hall until a wall of debris blocked his way and an open door to his right revealed a stairway. Taking it down, Hugh was greeted with a dank, pungent coolness. He was in the basement now, and he stopped, crouched and listening to the sound of dripping water echoing and hearing his own breath. This was the most dangerous part of his path back home—the Invaders loved the dark wetness. He knew two people who had been lost while traversing this short stretch, and had heard of at least a few more.

The basement was a huge area that ran under several of the buildings on 19th and had once served as a central plumbing hub. The only good thing about this room was that the large size made any sounds echo off the walls, alerting Hugh to movement. At the same time, the echoes made the location of such sounds hard to pin down, and the huge expanse was filled with old machinery and plumbing facilities providing too many good hiding places for the creatures. Waiting until he was satisfied that the room was quiet, Hugh swallowed, and stood. Using his light to guide the way, he followed the wall of pipes, splashing at times through unseen water that gave off a septic reek.

116

Hugh thought about Jaena. Not only did he miss her, but the memory of their times together gave him a respite from the painful reality of his current existence. He loved to reflect on those first months after they met and were getting to know each other. There was an unbridled sense of giddiness with every new discovery – the interests they shared, the movies they enjoyed, the books they discussed, even the walks they took all began to build into an overwhelming sense of joy and a feeling that this girl, finally, was the one.

Moving through the dank basement reminded Hugh of the day he introduced Jaena to his Live Action Role Playing group. In a room very similar to the one he had just traversed, she stood dressed in street clothes save for a cape and a Robin Hood-style hat borrowed from Hugh . Hugh had been dressed as an armor-clad warrior wearing metal pads that he had ordered from a catalog. Jaena had played the game very well that day and had been a great sport, but it was apparent that she did not like places like this: damp, dark and dirty.

Hugh smiled sadly at the memory. Reaching a place where the cinderblock wall was broken, he quickly stepped through to the stairwell beyond, and climbed to the relative safety of the floor above.

An empty doorway punctuated the hall and Hugh stopped. On the other side was the first checkpoint, meant to provide a first line of defense in the transition from the Infested Area to his little community of survivors' home base. Early on, they had learned the hard way that the creatures had the ability to home in on human voices making self-identification risky until they had found a new way to communicate their approach to the checkpoint.

Fishing in his pocket, Hugh withdrew a ballpoint pen which he clicked once, then twice. The faint sound was amplified by the emptiness around him and the deathly silence which hung in the air. While not failsafe, the "clicker" method was generally safer than simply calling out—perhaps the creatures found it harder to identify the source of sounds that were so quick, or perhaps they simply did not associate it with their human prey. A second later, he heard an answering click, telling him to proceed. At the far end shadows sat behind modified .50 caliber machine guns. One of them waved and Hugh waved back as he crossed the hall. It was to be the first of several lines of defense he'd go through as he drew closer to home.

Hugh wove his way through a maze of debris and passed by a boarded-up window. He took his hand off the grip of his rifle for the first time since that morning, tucked it under his arm and entered another hall. He was home now. A sliver of light peeked through the splintered wood covering the window and he peered through it, onto the street below. This was the time of day when commuters would have once been making their way home from a busy day at the office; now the gridlock sat frozen and silent, cars quietly dissolving where they had been abandoned those many years ago. After ten years he rarely thought back to those times, before the world fell, before the Invasion, but sometimes he remembered. Still, he knew it did no good to dwell on those memories—such thoughts could only make one crazy.

Hugh climbed to the upper stories of the brick building that he and the other survivors called home. He felt welcomed by the flurry of activity as men and women, the remaining few of their race, went about preparing for the night ahead. He could smell beans cooking—an aroma that signified home, though he couldn't pretend to relish the taste of beans themselves anymore, since they had been his daily fare for longer than he cared to remember. Hugh nodded greetings as he made his way to his room. Once there, he took a deep breath and leaned his rifle against the wall. He had made it through another day.

"We lost Greg today," a voice stated flatly from his door.

Hugh didn't have to turn to recognize that it was Wiley, their group's operations officer and general meddler. "Who?" Hugh asked as he began to strip off his layers of knapsack, satchels and belts.

"Greg Yi," Wiley said. "Over at the cathedral. Him and Bill were salvaging when they got jumped by squids. Bill made it, but Greg didn't. And it cost Bill an arm."

Hugh nodded grimly. Death was not as common now as it had been at the beginning, but grief was a commodity long past exhausted. It didn't pay to dwell on the losses they all had suffered—those who did stopped caring and then it was just a matter of time 'til they were gone too. He fished into one of his satchels and withdrew two unlabeled cans. "Dunno if these are any good, but there might be something worth salvaging," he told Wiley as he handed them over.

The older man took the cans and pointed to the book, poking out from the bag. "What's that?"

"Huh?" Hugh followed his gaze. "Oh, found that on my way back. Tolkien."

"Nice," Wiley grunted through a half-smile. "Sal's gonna enjoy adding that one to her collection."

Hugh pulled out the book and looked at it again, the memories of that long ago happenstance meeting in a bookstore still tickling. "Eventually. I think I wanna read it again first."

The other man shrugged and replied, "Sure. See you for dinner later?"

Hugh nodded and Wiley left. Exhausted, Hugh sat down on his cot, his bed for the past five years, and regarded the room around him. The cubby had served as an interior office for some law firm in the time before and it had no windows. He had compensated for the lack of a view by tacking up pictures found in his daily scrounging. Around him were views of a Washington, D.C. standing majestic, gleaming, in its marble finery on the shores of the Potomac.

Though they were pretty, looking at those photos sometimes gave him a sense of melancholy too. Nothing compared, though, to how he felt looking at the photo he carried of Jaena. It was the last thing he looked at before he went to bed and the first thing he looked at when he woke. It hurt to do so, but he needed it. Just because she wasn't with him anymore didn't mean he could just forget her.

Hugh knew that no relationship was ever perfect, but he sure felt like with Jaena they came close. Sure, there were little bumps in the road that any couple faced, particularly after they moved in together to that basement rental in Georgetown—small arguments over what TV shows to watch or how they were going to spend their vacation time, but with only one or two exceptions, the small stuff stayed small and even now Hugh smiled at the memory of how great things had been.

There had been a few big blow-ups though, ones that even now haunted Hugh during nights when sleep came slowly and he languished in a half-dream state.

The first had come after Jaena found out that Hugh had blown off studying for a midterm to attend an event with his gaming group. They had been walking around downtown and found themselves at Washington Circle park. Under the statue of the first president, Jaena expressed her disappointment, "Hugh, honestly I just don't get it. You're supposed to be a student first and play your games on the side. Is that really where your priorities lie?"

"I know," Hugh replied, "Sometimes I don't take the studying seriously enough—I know I need to do better."

Jaena shook her head, "You keep saying that, but you don't seem all that motivated to change. I mean, this isn't the first time you've done this sort of thing. To be honest, it makes me wonder what kind of boyfriend you'll make over the long-term. Will your gaming be more important than our relationship? You couldn't even go to my parent's 40th wedding anniversary last month because you had to go to GameCon in Chicago. Is that the way it's always going to be?"

"You're right, Jaena," he acknowledged.

"I'll be honest Hugh," she said "I think you should give it up."

"What?" Hugh recoiled. "What do you mean by that?"

"Give up the gaming, Hugh. It's time to grow up. You have so much potential; it's wasted on all these games."

Hugh grabbed a nearby park bench, "Jaena. You can't be serious."

"I am, Hugh."

That was their first, but not last, disagreement over the role of gaming in his life (or, "their life" as Jaena said). The irony was, the more overtly she frowned at it, the more tempted he was to seek refuge in that blameless fantasy world. Gaming, and the fantasy world surrounding it, brought a part of him alive that otherwise lay dormant and atrophied. Hugh never understood why Jaena couldn't simply be happy for him rather than feel angry. Even ten years later, he sometimes found himself dreading the self-recriminations that visited upon him at night as he lay in his cot—without Jaena and now his life like a science-fiction adventure gone bad.

The next morning Hugh and Lynn, a butchy woman from Gaithersburg, sat in the open doorway of their building looking out over the cluttered street. A bloated red sun cracked over the horizon, melting away the fog. Sweat had already started to form on Hugh's brow. For all that had changed in D.C. over the past decade, it sure hadn't lost its heat or humidity, he thought ruefully.

Their goal for the day was to get to Old Georgetown and back before nightfall. Rumor had it that there might be another group of survivors holed up at the university.

"You went there, right?" Lynn asked quietly as they prepared to move.

"Huh?" The question caught Hugh off-guard.

"The university. You were going to Georgetown when the shit hit the fan."

"Yeah."

Lynn nodded, readying her rifle and preparing to move. As the first rays of light poked through the blackened crowns of burnt-out buildings, the two sprinted across the street to the next row. After ten years, they had gotten used to the invader's ways and figured a thing or two out about them. Apparently, their eyesight was poor when the sun was low in the sky, so dawn and dusk were the best time for high-risk forays.

They were about to sprint to the next street when Hugh saw something. Past the ring of rusted cars sat the ruin of a familiar park. The statue of Washington now stood clothed in a robe of kudzu. Hugh flashed back to the day of the argument when Jaena had told him to quit gaming—it was as if he could see her standing beneath the monument amid the thick trees tell him to give up what he loved most. Hugh hesitated amidst his run, eyes narrowing at the turbulent memory of that terrible argument.

Lynn was on the other side of the block before she realized that she had lost Hugh. Turning around, she called out to him in a low but anxious voice "Hugh! C'mon!"

121

Hugh looked up at her note of urgency. He had stopped in the middle of the street—never a good place to be as that little dog had demonstrated just the day before. He ran, reaching the other side of the street where Lynn grabbed him roughly. "What is the matter with you?" she hissed and pointed down the street.

A long, black worm slithered among the cars.

For a moment, the beast, roughly twenty feet long and four feet thick, raised its ugly, tentacle-laden head above the ruined autos and seemed to sniff the air. Hugh and Lynn huddled in the corner of a collapsed building, hoping the smell of their fear and filth wouldn't reach its sensors. The worm was a patroller. While the other creatures slept, the patrollers made sure that nothing would disturb their rest. Hugh had long thought it ironically human-like. Every type of invader seemed to have a specialized job. There were ones who hunted, others who fought, and those who collected. He wondered if they had tax collectors too.

The invader slithered along the street, past the two humans hunched behind the fallen façade, and continued through the traffic circle. When it was clear, Lynn smacked Hugh in the arm. "What the hell was that?" she demanded in an angry voice.

"Nothing."

"What was so damn important to make you stop in the middle of a run like an idiot?"

Hugh wasn't sure himself, now. "I don't know—I got distracted."

"Was it about a girl?" Lynn asked. "Honey, it's been a long time for you, hasn't it?" She rolled her eyes, then smiled, forgiving him. "Don't make me save your sorry ass like that again, you hear?"

Clear-headed now, Hugh nodded. "Let's go."

They continued down Pennsylvania Avenue until the buildings gave way to a thick forest. Hugh hated going through Rock Creek Park—the invaders stood out among the hard lines and edges of man-made structures, but were near invisible in nature. And Hugh and Lynn had less than an hour left before the creatures would be moving again.

Midway through Rock Creek Park, a bridge remained intact over the old parkway. Several hundred meters in length, it was a long way to spring while completely exposed. Hugh started first as Lynn knelt at the end and kept watch, weapon ready.

"Hugh!" Lynn called just as a dark shadow appeared overhead. Hugh froze and saw one of the winged creatures far above, an apparent early riser. It circled above the bridge slowly, like a vulture making lazy circles in the sky. Hugh waited, hoping it had not perceived his movement. Tense moments later, the creature moved on up the parkway, moving along in its search for breakfast.

Lynn waited for him to get up and finish his run to the other side before making her own run under his watchful eye. "Wow," she said, "They're sure out and about today, aren't they?"

"Yeah," was all Hugh could say. He swallowed. "That was a close one." By mid-morning, the two had made it into Georgetown,not as far as they would have liked, but at least they were still alive. They entered a building with the weathered sign proclaiming it as the "_olde_ Swa_". Hugh nestled into the remains of a booth in what used to be the Golden Swan restaurant, while Lynn sat in the darkness covering the door. This was the place he and Jaena had gone to celebrate their one-year anniversary .

Looking over to a set of tables along the side of the room, Hugh remembered the night. Jaena had arrived late, her dark hair tied up in a ponytail and a package under her arm. She apologized as she sat down across from Hugh and slid him the wrapped present. "Hopefully this will make up for it."

He took the slender parcel and unwrapped it. It was a second edition *Dungeon & Dragons* manual. His eyes went wide and he grinned. Leaning across the table he kissed her cheek.

"How did you know to get me this?" He asked, turning the book over in his hands.

"I asked some of your gaming pals and they clued me in."

"This is amazing, Jaena—a real find. Thanks."

"Hugh?"

The voice was not Jaena's, but Lynn's. He snapped out of his reverie and saw that he was still in the restaurant, but it was in shambles, ruined and decaying. "We better push on if we're going to make it to the university and still get back before night."

Lynn was right. Hugh nodded, readied his rifle, and the two left the confines of the abandoned eatery.

They continued along M Street, where the road remained as choked with traffic as it had that fateful day. It was difficult to move now; cars were almost stacked. Even the sidewalks were clogged with the rusting junks of those unlucky many. They moved cautiously, covering one another as they leapfrogged up the street moving along the sidewalk as close to the edges of buildings as the traffic allowed. Pushing westwards, they approached the large, fortress-like buildings of Georgetown University.

As they began the final leg of their trek through a centuries-old neighborhood, Hugh felt a gnawing feeling in his stomach. Although it had been ten years, he still thought about Jaena every day, but she never stayed in his mind like this, distracting him with memories when he should be focused on survival.

In the quiet stillness of the approaching evening, Lynn and Hugh passed house after empty house. Doors and windows opened to the inky darkness of their interiors making for an unsettling scene. As they sat for a moment at the base of a fallen oak tree, Hugh looked and saw a house just like the row house that housed their basement apartment. Voices from his memory resonated as if he could still hear them clearly from the open window.

Hugh looked at Lynn, who was watching down the street and drinking from her canteen. "I'll be right back," he whispered to her and took off for the house.

"What?" She turned. "Where you going? Hugh? Get back here!"

Lynn's words followed him as he passed through the gaping entrance of the nondescript row-house and was enveloped by the coolness of the shadowy interior. At his feet were some weathered newspapers opened to the comics section. The day came roaring back as if he was there.

"Hugh!" he heard Jaena's voice. "I can't believe you, Hugh!"

Hugh could see her at the top of the stairs. Jaena was mad—the angriest that he had ever seen her, in fact. It was the second anniversary of their first date and he had forgotten all about it. He had been invited to a comic book convention by some friends and didn't know anything was wrong until he came home to find Jaena wrapped in a thrall of tearful injury.

"You and your fantasy world, Hugh!" she cried, and flung a 1933 edition of *Weird Tales* at him. "I'll always be on the sideline, won't I?!"

"No! It's not like that, I'm so sorry Jaena!!" he told her, frantically trying to put the comic back into its protective wrapper.

"Yes it is, Hugh! You'd rather spend your time with your buddies, Lovecraft and Bradbury!"

"Don't say that, sweetie!" Hugh begged as he dodged a re-release of *The Shadow Over Innsmouth*. "I just forgot! It'll never happen again, I swear!"

Jaena took down a collected works anthology and with a final bout of anger, threw it straight at Hugh's head. There was no impact, though. Hugh looked up into the empty room at the top of the stairs and wondered what had just happened.

"Hugh!" Lynn's voice called from the front door. "What is wrong with you man? Stop acting crazy!"

He rejoined his partner out front.

"I guess I'm a little distracted today," Hugh admitted, unnerved by the memory.

But before Lynn could respond, she was gone. The black creature had snatched her from the sidewalk before Hugh could blink. He heard her screaming and stared helplessly as she was lifted into the sky by one of the squids. Shock rooted Hugh in place. The sound of her rifle crashing on the street jolted him into action.

Hugh ran west in the direction of the university. He knew the creatures would be back looking for him. Out of breath, he took a break in a corner store. His world had fallen the day the Invaders arrived. Ten years later, he was still getting used to the hell that had become day-to-day life. But even with the constant tragedy and fear, there was a status quo about it. Now, every time he turned a corner he had some memory of Jaena if all that had happened yesterday, not a decade ago.

A car pulled up out front and honked as he ran along the edge of Holy Trinity school. He looked and saw Jaena's blue Honda. *It's not there*, Hugh told himself, *just in your head.*

She honked again and he heard her call, "C'mon! We'll be late!"

He remembered it now. They'd been heading to class at the university when he popped the question. It all came rushing back—the smell of her car, the rain falling on the windshield, the press of the ring box in his pocket. He had wanted to surprise her at home, but with both of them taking classes and studying well into the night, there was never the right moment. He got into the car and before she could pull away from the curb, he quietly took the box from his pocket and opened it in front of her.

Jaena stared at the ring for a minute and looked up into his face. A tremulous smile broke out on her face. "Really, Hugh?" she asked. Hugh took the ring out of the box and held it out to her. They had been through some hard times together, in fact it was in the aftermath of the fight after he missed their anniversary that he had resolved to ask. "I'm going to make you ask" she said. He saw a tear gathering in her eye and knew then that she'd say yes.

Hugh had saved to buy it. He'd gone without finishing his collection of *Weird Tales* and *Amazing Stories* magazines. It was all worth it to know that they would share the rest of their lives together.

They never made it to class that night; instead, they went home to celebrate. It was a humid, rainy summer night; and it was the best night of his life.

Not quite knowing how he got there, Hugh found himself standing on the corner of O and 37th with the imposing brick fortress of Healy Hall looming up from the trees ahead of him. For the past several years, there had been rumors of survivors hiding among the ruins and below in the tunnel systems, but every search had turned up nothing.

Just below that lone tower, however, a he saw a dim light from the top floor, confirming the reports. The last time Hugh had set foot on the campus was the day of the Invasion. It was the day after he proposed to her, and what followed the best day of his life turned into the most tragic.

Hugh, books in hand, bounded down the stairs—he was running late. English class had been slow that day and he had just struggled through a Calculus mid-term. He was glad to be done for the day.

Hugh heard his name called as he left the building for the parking lot. He turned to see Jaena coming up beside him. They kissed. Jaena, excited about their engagement, played with the ring on her finger. She looked at him and said, "Why wait for a big to-do? Let's just elope."

"Really?" Hugh asked. He hadn't been hoping for a big wedding himself, but the suddenness of the idea took him off guard. "Ok! When do you want to do it, then?"

"What about today?" she asked, poking him playfully.

"Ummm...I have D&D with the guys later this afternoon...maybe tomorrow?" He looked at her face and knew that he'd given the wrong answer. She stood, looking at him, eyes growing red and with a stricken look on her face. Suddenly she began to twist the ring off her finger. "Honey, I love the idea of eloping; it's just...can't we do it tomorrow instead?" he asked. As she opened her mouth to answer, the ground shook. A moment later the ground shook again. And again. Students stopped and looked to one another uncertainly. Soon, people poured out of the building and gathered in small groups, as if seeking the security of the company of strangers. A crowd gathered in the Student Center where a television was showing live coverage of events that seemed... unreal... impossible...except that by now they were beginning to happen on campus too. Fires were burning in several buildings. Shadowy creatures bounded in and out of view. People were snatched by things in the sky. Uncertainty turned into panic as students and teachers fled the university.

Explosions began to roil the city. Military helicopters flew in formations overhead, engaging an invisible enemy.

The sky was filled with strange, nightmarish creatures that plunged from the clouds and swooped up people from the street.

Giant black snakes slithered from the sewers, grabbing others and dragging them down. The Invasion had begun.

Jaena and Hugh ran. He did not know where they were going, perhaps towards home. Suddenly, one of the flying creatures snatched up Jaena and flew away into the smoke-filled air. Hugh screamed "Jaena! Jaena!" and ran after the shrinking shape of the creature carrying his beloved into the broken sky. Soon she was gone from sight and he was left on the street alone. Hugh ran on, as if still hoping to catch her. He caught his foot on a curb at the edge of the street, tripped, and sprawled into a crater. Down and down his body rolled, feeling as though it would never hit the bottom.

The doctor looked through the small window to view his patient. Hugh was curled up in a ball against the padded walls of his cell in St. Elizabeth's Hospital. Next to the doctor was a nurse, new to the hospital, carrying a clipboard. "Patient 109845," the doctor told her, "Hugh Wilson. Age 20. Arrived the 16th of August in a catatonic state after he collapsed in the midst of an argument with his girlfriend. Described by friends and family as shy, above-average intelligence, and a little out of touch. His ex-girlfriend still visits him from time to time, and is quoted as saying that he 'lived in his head a lot' and was having ever more frequent episodes of disassociation before the collapse.

"Since arrival, subject has failed to engage and overall shown little improvement. Family recently opted to discontinue electro-convulsive therapy. We keeping him on a maintenance program of 2 mg of Lorazepam for the time being. To be honest, I'm really not sure that the ex-girlfriend's visits help—seems like he ratchets a notch down every time."

Couriers

Lorri Stone

During Amelia's Metro ride home from the National Botanical Gardens in Washington D.C., she passed the time in her usual way: she daydreamed about killing strangers on the train.

The dozing man in a grubby maintenance uniform she chose to smother with a pillow as he slept. The sweaty young man in an expensive suit she would throw onto the tracks and wait to see if he died from the electricity in the third rail before the train could smear him. The skinny teenage boy hunched over his phone Amelia decided to stab in the head with a barbecue fork. Should she impale his sullen, spotty face through an eye socket, or perhaps through the roof of his mouth? Would she need a hammer?

She changed trains at L'Enfant Plaza. Clutching her cheap messenger bag in front of her, Amelia scurried through the rush hour crowd to the blue line platform. It was nearly empty after her errand in the city, but still she gripped it as tightly as if it was full of diamonds. Courier duty was the most mundane part of her work but Amelia took it very seriously. The delivery was vital to the goal.

During the subway part of the commute, she focused on turning her personal space into an impenetrable shell. She hated and feared the herd of humanity surrounding her, but she'd learned long ago that letting her repulsion show caused trouble. If she made eye contact and allowed someone to see her hatred, the person would probably take it personally. Even if they didn't, they would remember her, and she treasured her anonymity. So Amelia never looked higher than anyone's shoulder.

South. After a brief eternity, the train reached the end of the line. Amelia thronged with the animals to the escalators, clutching her bag and staring stonily at the back of the woman in front of her. She carefully estimated the position of the pair of ribs she'd have to miss with her imaginary knife when she

129

stabbed the anonymous woman to death. Her fingers shifted slightly as she mentally spun the blade to lie flat before sliding it between the bones.

Amelia stumped across the parking lot towards her car, breathing a little easier as the swarm dispersed. She knew the rest of her trip down I-95 would be tense, but at least she wouldn't be able to smell anyone or have to listen to their grunts and yammers once she was alone in her car. She thought with horror of what it would be like to live inside the District and be swamped by these hideous people all the time. The required monthly trips into the city were hellish, but the rest of the time she spent in the house she'd grown up in, a small brick island in a moat of scrappy woods almost in the center of sixteen acres in Stafford County, VA. Its verdant solitude comforted her.

The single story ranch house squatted under the unkempt trees. Ivy climbed the walls without adding any country-house charm; the wild growth made the place look forbidding, like a jungle ruin. The remains of the flower garden were lush with weeds and ivy. The front door was nearly covered by huge boxwoods.

A greenhouse stood in a small clearing that was once part of the back yard, but was now colonized by young pines and tulip poplars. A clear footpath led from the back door to the plastic frame shed. Ivy grew up the corners of this building also, but the shed did not look dingy and neglected; this place was clearly in constant use. A long orange extension cord followed the path and powered the lights dimly visible through the dirty plastic walls.

Amelia parked behind the house and used the back door. There was another plain, worn dirt path in the wild grass between her usual parking place and the entrance. The wind rustled soothingly in the trees and the rich living scent of moist earth welcomed her.

A note was rolled up and stuck between the knob and the frame. Amelia frowned at it, but took it inside. She lowered her bag gently to the floor as she read:

tonight
D

Beside the words was a drawing that looked something like a lost game of hangman: a stick man dangling from a stick tree instead of a stick gallows.

"Finally!" Amelia's frown lifted at once. She plucked an apple from a bowl on the counter and crunched it happily. The little snack would do for now, especially since she knew dinner was going to be extra special tonight.

Dale carried the heavy duffel bag out of the cellar and tossed it into the back of the truck with an effortless swing. His brother Matt looked down from the roof of the house, nails in his mouth, and a new shingle in his hand. They nodded at each other and shared a comfortable, friendly glance.

Dale went back inside for a minute to see to the cellar. It was clean and tidy, with the big empty dog crates stacked against the wall and the tool bench organized. Matt always made a pigsty out of the place, but he sure did clean it up good when he was done. It was one of the reasons the brothers still made such companionable roommates. Each had his own habits and quirks but was careful to mind the other's pet peeves and sore spots. Matt was a slob on his own, but Dale was not, so while Matt's room stayed smelly and filthy he cleaned up behind himself down here in the space they shared. The two of them were alike in everything important. Now that they were grown they didn't fight about small stuff.

Matt's side had the crates and tools as well as rope coiled neatly on ceiling hooks and an old camping cot with a faded blanket tossed over it. There was only a bare bulb over the bench. It was good enough; Dale's side of the cellar was mostly full of his indoor garden and the special plant lights were bright.

He paused to gaze at his plants with loving care. The third one from the left was looking much healthier today. Its leaves were waxy, pliant and richly green. Dale was pleased to see it was doing better on its special food, but he knew the soil was becoming depleted. He'd take care of that soon.

Locking the door carefully behind him, Dale went back out to the truck, whistling. He picked up an old five-gallon paint bucket from the back shed and a mismatched lid that fit and tossed them into the cab through the open passenger side window.

He called up to Matt, "Prolly won't be home tonight."

Matt grinned at him. "Have fun!"

Dale saw to it that the duffel bag was secure and couldn't move around before climbing behind the wheel. He examined himself in the rear view mirror and smoothed his hair, then huffed into his palm to check his breath and popped a mint.

He heard laughter, and saw Matt watching him from above. Dale laughed too, cheerfully flipped his brother the finger, and drove away.

Dale arrived at the crazy girl's house and switched off his headlights. The dirty glow of the greenhouse was the only illumination. Deep twilight was succumbing to full darkness under the trees. He unloaded his duffel bag and his empty bucket and trudged to the plastic door. After pausing to take a few deep calming breaths, he swung the bucket to knock on a support pole.

The light went out. While his eyes adjusted, Dale heard the door open and close. Amelia nestled against him in the darkness and stroked him through his clothes. She smelled like rich earth and mown grass. Dale shivered. Who cared if the crazy bitch worshipped plants or whatever the fuck she did?

She stepped away and lit a heavy flashlight. Her messenger bag hung over her shoulder, but other than that she was wearing only a thin shapeless dress barely more concealing than a long t-shirt. Her silhouette ahead of him as they went into the woods was all he could look at, and he stumbled behind her more than once before they reached the clearing.

Amelia stepped to the side and shone the light on the great gnarled tree that dominated the dirt-floored circle. Its black bark was deeply creased and fuzzed over with moss. Thick shelves of gray-brown fungus protruded randomly. If the two of them had stretched their arms around the trunk, their fingertips might touch. A huge limb reached out above them and nearly crossed the width of the clearing. Nowhere was there a green leaf, but somehow the bare tree was plainly fetid with life.

Amelia put the bag down beside her and knelt on the dirt. She pulled off the thin dress and tossed it aside, prostrating herself before the tree. Her whispered prayer sank into to the black earth.

Dale stared hungrily at her. Then he dropped the bag and wrenched it open. A young man rolled out onto the dirt.

He was also naked, terribly thin and pale. His mutilated hands and feet were wrapped with bloody rags and bound together with duct tape. He was not gagged, but he made no sound. His skin was a sickly mass of wounds and his eyes were dull pebbles in his beaten face.

Rising to her feet, Amelia began to chant a series of guttural, ugly syllables. From her bag she withdrew a worn kitchen knife. The flashlight she propped against a rotten log to illuminate the clearing with its sharp beam, creating deep shadows.

Dale pulled a rope from the bag and tossed one end over the tree's scarred limb. Quickly he knotted it around the catatonic young man's neck. Then stepping back he hauled on the other end of the rope until the thin figure dangled just above the ground. He tied the rope on a nearby rock. Dale roughly yanked his clothes off as Amelia's chant buzzed in the silent woods.

Except for a change in his breathing, the young man did not react to being hanged. His eyes did not follow Amelia's movement as she approached him, flashlight in one hand, knife in the other. His time as a prisoner in Dale and Matt's basement had already destroyed his mind.

Amelia's words were unintelligible to Dale as he watched from his knees nearby, but there was no doubt what she was saying. Even the air seemed thick with supplication as she sang her hatred and longing into the night. Visions swam before his eyes of the city tumbling to rubble in the grip of rampant green, and human corpses softening into loam to feed the conquering foliage.

As she chanted, she carefully carved a small strip of flesh from the young man's body. She lifted it high and squeezed it in her fist making blood drip onto her face. She popped the scrap into her mouth. Amelia savored it before swallowing, and resumed the song with a blissful look on her face.

Amelia tossed another butchered strip to Dale. He caught it in one hand and ate it greedily. Blood splattered his chin and chest.

The young man's eyes stayed unfocused and dim as Amelia carved and ate him. Blood ran freely down his dangling body. His face was turning deep red-purple as he labored to breathe against the strangling rope but he did not struggle.

Amelia raised the knife above her head as her chant reached the crescendo. Then she gutted him.

For the first time, an emotion appeared in the dull eyes. An expression of relief flickered briefly on his face as his life escaped.

Triumphantly, Amelia offered her sacrifice to the fecund, conquering green. She was slick with the young man's blood. Wet piles of indescribable tubes and lumps slithered to the ground, soaking the dirt.

Under her feet the soil rippled queasily. Nearby, the flashlight wobbled and rolled off its log, shining its light away from the desecration in the clearing.

Dale sprang forward and dragged Amelia down to the bloody dirt. Her chant became laughter and wordless cries. Dale's ferocious rutting seemed to take up where her chanting left off and his grunts continued the inhuman song. Only a flailing foot or a thrown clod of mud was visible in the skewed flashlight beam as the dirt beneath them roiled like a stew.

The soaking earth parted and gnarled roots began to rise. The wobbling light sent their hideous shadows careening crazily through the woods. Thin creeping tendrils and huge twisted limbs broke free of the blood-soaked ground and moved out of view with blind hunger towards Amelia and Dale.

Amelia was awake and busy by the time Dale finally opened his eyes. She grinned at him as he struggled to get up. He was plainly sore in every fiber, and groaned as he moved. This amused her. Amelia never felt better than she did the morning after a ceremony. Obviously Dale was not chosen by the green. He was useful for now, however.

She hummed happily to herself as she carefully collected the dirt sanctified by the ritual into Dale's bucket and plastic peanut butter jars. The gory mess was gone. The body of the young man was also gone, with only a shredded rope end dangling over the heavy limb to show where he had been. The huge tree's roots were no longer visible. Its branches hung silently overhead and the parasitic growths on the trunk slept. Everything smelled rich and alive and the light of a new dawn filled the clearing with patient beauty.

Dale stumbled but reached his pile of discarded clothes without falling. Getting dressed was a slow ordeal, and Amelia had time to finish her task before he was done. When they left the clearing, it was hard to imagine anything had happened there.

He loaded his heavy bucket of damp dirt and his empty duffel bag into his truck. Amelia carried her bag of jars into the greenhouse. They parted without a word. Both of them had plants to feed.

In his basement, Dale carefully packed the fresh, rich soil around the roots of his hybrids. He tossed each one of them a bit of the young man's dismembered fingers so they wouldn't bite him as he worked.

In her greenhouse, Amelia freshened the soil of her huge potted flowers and harvested the first of next month's delivery of pollen. As she gathered the pale powder, she smirked with haughty disdain for the unimaginative minds of the terrorists who were content to kill only a portion of humanity. Anthrax, indeed. Amateurs.

Dupont Underground
CAT

She had been stalking him for weeks now. She wanted to confirm her suspicions before confronting him, but she was fairly certain that the broad shouldered, kind-eyed night nurse from the VA hospital was an angel.

Tonight would be the third time she had followed him home and she was grateful for his regular habits. After his shift, he took the Metro back toward the city. He exited at the Dupont Circle Station and stopped at the same Starbucks for the same drink – some disgustingly sweet confection with whipped cream and drizzles of chocolate and caramel. He would smile at the same transgender barista and – no matter how crudely the drink was made – tip a dollar.

Spotting her, he would nod or smile or raise his cup. That's how she noticed him; he greeted everyone. As he left, he would say something pleasant, turn, and exit. Then, he would walk along the dark streets toward Georgetown to his apartment where he would draw the blinds, toss his PBA-free commuter mug in the sink, shower, pray, and sleep.

Usually, come Saturday, he would wake at 5am and head off to volunteer all morning at Bread for the City and then all afternoon at the Whitman-Walker AIDS clinic. This weekend, they would have to do without him. The Monday holiday would give her an extra day before anyone knew he was missing.

Getting him alone would be risky but she had a plan - confront him, lay out her case, straight out ask for his help, and not get killed. That was the plan. The hard part would be getting him to help her, considering she was a vampire.

She waited outside his apartment until she could hear his heart slow with sleep. "Pull yourself together," she said aloud, hesitating to enter. The ancient tongue would only have sounded like distant music to any neighbor who might have heard her.

She stopped twisting her fingers and laid her hands flat on the door. She was grateful for its wooden core because, after she broke in on him, she could hardly ask to feed from him to regain her strength. She pressed her hands against the door, wishing for a time when she would be older, stronger, and it would hurt less to pass through objects. "Cheap particle board," she thought as she emerged on the other side.

His tiny studio was spartan – one cup, one plate, one spoon, one knife, one fork, Shaker furniture, white curtains. Even the guitar leaning against the foot of his bed was simple. Only the cheerfully colored commuter cup in the sink seemed out of place with its red ribbon on a field of black.

She picked up his wallet and examined his drivers' license. Out of all of the names in all of the tongues of man, he had taken the name "Paiste," Gaelic for "child." He did have a remarkably handsome photo though. He had $14 in cash but no credit cards – only a library card and a METRO pass.

"Hello, hello, hello, William," the vampire sighed. Tucked behind the license was a picture of a woman, a plain-looking Army captain of about 30. On the back, it read, "CAPT Dana Michele Roberts, KIA 19 February 1991." Dead since the first Gulf War, Dana was not exactly his girlfriend. She replaced his wallet on the table.

She crossed a patch of rug to the bookcase full of religious works – the Bhagavad Gita in Sanskrit, mystic texts in Hebrew, a Bible in Swahili, Japanese meditation verses, a photo essay on Yosemite, a book of quantum physics. She moved to the closet and opened it to find his Marine Corps uniform. She bit her lip. "Fuck me," she said aloud and closed the door quickly. He was one of Michael's soldiers. That explained the VA. She half-expected the Archangel himself to appear and kill her.

A few feet away, the angel slept. Stretched out on his back and half-tangled in a sheet, he looked like a figure from some church's ceiling but less androgynous. He looked like a man. Maybe what she knew of angels was as wrong as what humans knew of her kind. Maybe they needed sleep. Maybe waking him would end her time on earth. She cursed her indecision. She was running out of time.

She perched on the foot of his bed – hoping to avoid his reach – and leaned across him. He smelled intoxicating. "Hey," she said, touching his leg with her icy fingers. "Wake up."

In a heartbeat, the angel was on his feet. He looked bewildered but he recognized her. "What are you doing here?"

He looked at the closed door. A faint scent of sawdust floated in the air. "How did you get in?"

She addressed him in the ancient language. "Do you know what I am, 'Child?'"

The angel hissed at her, "Go back to Hell, demon." His gaze went to the closet.

She had not checked for weapons. "Threats of damnation don't work on vampires."

Backing slowly away from her toward the kitchenette, the angel began to pray, "Michael, brother and Archangel, be my defense…"

"Please!" She pleaded, raising her hands. "I need your help to save a life."

The angel looked at her and laughed.

The angel and the vampire walked up R St. past the Oak Hill cemetery through Georgetown toward Dupont Circle. In the moonlight, his blond hair looked blue.

They passed elegant gardens of roses, hydrangeas, and ornamental shrubs. The roots of trees occasionally cast ripples in the brick sidewalk held in check by granite curbs.

"Why 'Paiste?'"

"A drummer's joke - noisy cymbal, noisy child. Child of God." He hooked his thumbs in the back pockets of his jeans. "'Zildjian' sounds like a robot." He laughed at his own joke. "Where exactly are we going?"

"It's called the 'Dupont Underground,'" the vampire explained. "Before DC had buses, there were streetcars. Under the park at Dupont Circle but above the train tracks for the METRO, there is an abandoned streetcar terminal and a series of tunnels. They started building it after WWII, finished it in 1949, and then abandoned it at the start of 1962 when the city went to buses." She drew a map in the air. "There were three underground stops before the streetcars emerged south on Connecticut Avenue over by N or M Street. The old station was underneath the intersection of Connecticut Avenue and S Street."

"So I walk over a vampire hive every day?" He had seen

the boarded-up entrances by the bank and the Krispy Kreme but never thought about it.

The angel paused at one massive tree as he passed, life boiling out of the ground amid broken bricks. He took a deep breath and laid a hand on it, "Strength for your fight, old spirit."

A warm May wind stirred the dogwood blossoms. The conversation paused as they walked. He enjoyed the pleasant silence. She was distracted; for an angel, he smelled tantalizingly like food.

"I thought demons could fly," he said.

"Vampire," she replied. "I'm not nearly old enough to fly but I can do this." She jumped up on the wall of the cemetery in an effortless bound, balanced for a second, and threw herself down.

The angel lunged to break her fall but just as she would have been dashed on the bricks, she exploded upward to hang in the air, her feet even with his waist. She descended slowly to a soft landing in front of him. She twirled around and curtsied. "Fall but miss the ground."

The angel applauded, "That was beautiful."

"No more tricks. I need my strength to push you through the ground."

"You need to what?"

"Later," she said. "For the record, I thought angels could fly. And why do you speak in human tongues?"

"I am human..."

"What?" She stopped in her tracks and issued a blood-curdling ancient curse. Birds fell from the sky and the flowers on the tree turned brown and shriveled. Her lip curled into a snarl and she started to pace. "Fuck me, fuck me, fuck me..."

"Bless you," said the angel. "I can still understand the ancient tongue but I must speak in the tongues of man sequentially – not all at once. Not like before." *Part of the punishment, he thought.*

She turned to face him. "Can you still heal?"

"I am a nurse."

139

Turning south on 28th Street, they walked on while she fumed, muttering curses under her breath. Spring curdled brown behind her.

"Stop ruining the landscaping," the angel said. "You're like a plague of locusts."

The vampire sulked in silence. As they came to the Q St. bridge, she stopped at the buffalo sculpture and leaned on the plinth. "How did this happen?"

"I saved a life."

In the waning days of the Persian Gulf War came the liberation of Kuwait called Desert Storm. On the outskirts of Kuwait City, CAPT Dana Roberts, an Army medic, was tending to an American soldier and an Iraqi insurgent in a small tent at an understaffed MASH unit. The Perfect Plan dictated that, as Roberts worked on the American, the young Iraqi would wake, grab his pistol from the side table, and shoot her and his enemy dead – only to be killed by those responding to the scene.

The angel, sent to return souls to heaven, appeared to the medic in the body of a Marine he had slain moments before. She could not know that she was supposed to die.

As Roberts scissored off the remainder of the American's pants, she spoke to the soldier, "Lieutenant Garcia, you're not dying today. The 'O+' on your boots saved your life – unlucky or not." She looked up as the angel entered the tent.

"Where you been, Sergeant? Two units oh-pos and morphine," she ordered him. Elbow deep in the American's blood, she was making an attempt to clamp his femoral artery. "We can save them both."

The angel witnessed her treat each casualty with an equal measure of skill and kindness. In all of time, he had never encountered a human soul who so loved mankind. Her desire to heal was so strong.

In that moment, he loved her.

When Roberts turned to reach for more gauze, the angel laid his hand on the Army lieutenant and healed the soldier's wounds. Garcia glimmered toward waking but the angel ran a hand over him saying, "Peace." Garcia slept.

At that moment, the insurgent awakened, recovered his pistol, and fired but the angel shielded Roberts from the bullet.

Enraged, the angel jumped over gurney and grabbed the Iraqi by the throat. "I would have saved you," he said. A thousand tiny wounds burst from the man's skin, his body arched. The Iraqi screamed.

It was then that Michael, general of the army of angels, appeared. The Archangel raised his hand and the Iraqi fell silent and still. Garcia's leg split open. Sprays of bright red blood painted the tent's tan ceiling; the man convulsed and died. CAPT Roberts snatched up a scalpel to defend herself. Michael gestured to her. The medic put the blade to her throat and cut across her neck. She fell to her knees, gurgling.

"She is damned because of you," Michael hissed. Demons appeared, swirling in the corners of the tent and reaching with black, smoky tendrils toward the disoriented souls.

"No," the angel grabbed his general by the arm, putting Michael's hand over his own heart. He stared into his brother's eyes. "I surrender to her my place in heaven to her."

Michael smiled. "Thy will be done."

The angel lost control of the borrowed body as Michael lifted him up by the shirt. A cold sensation spread through the angel's borrowed body, the arms flopped back separating both shoulders with a gristly pop. He felt his back rip open, the skin splitting under his shoulder blades. The Archangel dropped him in a heap on the ground.

There was a second of blackness followed by the nauseating pull of gravity. He opened new eyes to Roberts' lifeless body a few feet away his – empty eyes and open mouth asking why – as her blood seeped toward him. Michael towered above him in a spotless Army uniform – a borrowed body. He kicked the angel in the shoulder and led the woman's soul away.

Then, he was screaming and life began on earth.

"Over a woman," she said. "Fuck me."

"Bless you," he corrected.

"Fuck you." She smiled at him.

"I made a choice," he said. "But I am *not* God."

She could not interpret the tone in his voice or the look on his face. She had no experience with the thousand-yard stare of a weary soldier. They walked in silence again until she burst out, "I thought God was about free will..."

"In humans," he said. "The heavenly host is supposed to obey."

"But... you're the good guys."

"And Michael is the best. Chronicles 21:15 'The Lord sent an angel to destroy Jerusalem. As the angel was rendering them, the Lord grieved for the destruction and cried, 'Enough! Stay your hand.' Destroying the city was some of Michael's best work." The angel kicked a rock over the bridge. Below, Rock Creek and Potomac Parkway was utterly deserted. "You are made in the image of the Lord and some of you are paranoid schizophrenics... ever wonder about that?"

"Is that why you work with the junkies and the trannies and schizophrenics and what not when you're not working with half-fuck broken soldiers?"

"It's not so simple. God is like all of them, in all of them." He looked up at the clouds obscuring the sky. "There is no salvation for angels – check your holy books. I don't know if my prayers are ignored or not, but I can still help people by living among them, giving my life for them in a small way." The angel laughed again. He extended a hand and pulled her to her feet.

"That sounds... " She sputtered over a word.

"Hey, Jesus did it. Mohammad, the Buddhas, the Dalai Lamas, Mother Teresa... of course, I had the GI bill."

He put an arm around her. For a second, her head rested on his shoulder. He was strong and warm and smelled of masculinity. Though she wanted to stay there, she extricated herself, gnawing with hunger. *Focus.*

The vampire sighed and gave the buffalo an affectionate pat. "I remember when these went in. It was about 10 years before I was turned. Everyone was nostalgic for the old west. The buffalo nickel had just come out and, here in the District, Alexander Phimister Proctor was putting an animal on every bridge. I loved art and architecture when I lived."

They walked across the bridge, down the little side street toward P St., then up P St. toward the circle.

She stopped in front of the Hotel Palomar. "I was turned not far from here. Once upon a time, here sat the grand Pelham Apartments. One Harrison Gray Dyar, Jr. nearly killed me as I emerged from the ground. I'll have to tell you the whole story one day."

They continued east until they reached the white marble fountain. The vampire pointed out that it was a memorial to Samuel Francis DuPont who was once a Rear Admiral in the U.S. Navy. "They put this here when the original statue was moved to Wilmington. It was designed by Daniel Chester French and Henry Bacon. They did the Lincoln memorial too. It's even carved by the same Italian marble smiths – the Piccirilli family."

They walked a slow circle around the fountain as moonlight reflected off figures of the wind, sea, and stars.

"Human imperfection," the angel said. Water flowed out of only one of the three spouts.

"I won't kid you," she said. "This is going to hurt." She exhaled a rotting fruit scent he had long associated with evil. Her eyes glowed. "Sorry about this."

She bit her wrist and sucked some of the blood. Drawing his face down to hers, she kissed him and pushed the blood into his mouth. He had no time to feel repulsed by the metallic taste. The Dupont Circle fountain shimmered as the intoxicant spread through his body. His legs itched.

Then, they were falling. They plunged through the ground, through concrete, through wood, through wires and plaster and nothing. He thought they might suffocate and die but he did not care. He wanted to tell her this was just like Valium but, curiously, he could not speak. All his bones were breaking.

They slammed through the ceiling in a cavernous, white-tiled room and onto a concrete slab - one side of a train platform with a tunnel that stretched out into darkness. People and shadows swarmed around them, speaking the ancient words. He had never heard so many voices since he was in heaven. Someone called for Adam.

"I know Adam," the angel thought.

The vampire looked ill - not pale, but ashen grey. He could smell her rotting. Adam, a young man with multiple piercings, pushed through the crowd. He had the vampire's wavy black hair and pale skin. Though thin and as poorly dressed as a clinic patient, Adam appeared remarkably healthy. The vampire fell on the boy, slashing into his neck and drinking. Blood sprayed up in the air and spilled across the boy's chest.

The angel was appalled. Nausea welled up in him at the scent of blood and garbage. Woozy, he tried to take a step. The voices whispered around him, "So beautiful." "Who is he?" "First time…" "Catch him, catch him!" someone said. He had no intention of running. Then, he realized he was going to faint.

""Wake up." She was on top of him again. "Blood makes you a little stupid at first."

Her eyes were so green. "*Luminous*," he thought. Finding his tongue, he said, "You're luminous."

"Shock him."

"Not… dead…" he wanted to say.

A pasty-looking, bald man leaned over him with the kind of defibrillator used for cardiac arrest. Pain seared through his body and the fog in his head replaced by a deep throbbing sensation. Slowly, he realized that he was lying in his boxers on a gurney in a state-of-the-art surgical suite.

"Get up." She held out a glass of water to him. "What do you know about hardening?"

"It's an evil your kind perpetrates on man." He sat up on the table. The water tasted amazing. Sure, Jesus had turned it into wine, but he understood the potential of the stuff now, the life force. He examined the glass. It was like drinking happiness. He inhaled the scent of it and drained the glass, surprised by the pleasure of it.

"It's a *process* our kind uses to create those who protect us." She explained the process of creating a guardian by exchanging a small amount of blood between a chosen human and several vampires. "We select those who are already strong or swift or gifted and we make them better. Some, like Adam, turn into feeders. Some become guardians or enclave guards. Some… well, some fail."

"Fail how?"

"They develop our appetites without our impulse control. They turn on everything and kill - animals, humans, and vampires alike. They are sociopaths, rapists, and eventually serial killers." She shrugged. "We do not condone hardening beyond a certain point but the government keeps a few of us on staff to harden Navy SEALS and the like. I hear some of them can actually take a bullet and live."

"The coffee was for your guardian?"

"We're not evil," she said. "We want to make antibodies using your blood." She handed pink and purple-capped vials of blood to the man who had shocked him. "Giles... he's sort of our mob doctor here in the Underground. He thinks he can help the ones who have hardened too much. Make them more... human."

Giles turned over the vampire's wrist. While it was already healing, he put a red paste on it and then wiped it away. The wound was gone. He gave the vampire a long meaningful look and shrugged. He drew an ornate bracelet out of his pocket and fastened it to her wrist. She winced.

The child of God sat silent for a long time then said, "How do we start?"

"We already have. I will exchange blood with you another few times in the next few hours. Giles will do some analysis." She turned toward the lab tech. "Go back to the lab, Giles." Then, she said something in a language he did not understand. The only word he got sounded like "Adam." Giles slipped through the double doors that must have once led away from the platform.

"Is Adam okay?"

"He's fine." The vampire twisted her fingers.

He let the lie pass. "How come I couldn't understand what you said?"

"It's the language of Sammael and the defectors."

At least that was true; the language of the damned was the only language an angel could not understand. "Sammael..." the words died in his mouth, *"He Who is Like God."* Sammael had been like a brother to him before the fall, but Sammael was also a warrior and a trickster. While never outright evil, he was difficult. Moses himself had prayed to be delivered from this angel. "Is he here?"

The vampire drew near and rested her cold hand on his shoulder. "You need to regenerate a little. There are clothes in the closet. Get dressed. This is a club after all."

The closet was stocked like a Goth kid's dream. The angel selected a black t-shirt, a black silk button-down shirt, and dark denim jeans. He looked at himself in the mirror hanging from the back of the closet door. "I look like a tough."

"Here," the vampire said, handing him a pair of black Italian loafers. "These should fit."

They did.

Across the trolley platform, he saw people writhing together. At first, he thought it was some kind of torture, but then he saw they were dancing. A section of what once was a food court now functioned as a disco. The vampire beckoned. In her short black dress, she looked like a celebrity party girl.

"I don't hear any music."

"You will." She held out a red-black capsule in one hand and a glass of water in the other. "Take it."

His body tingled. The vampire's black dress began to sparkle. Then, he heard it. If there could be hip-hop in Hell, this was it. Slowly, the music got louder until his whole body reverberated with it. They joined the dance.

"What's your name?" he shouted.

"Moira. Funny you picked a Gaelic name."

"I can no longer say my real name," he said. "How old are you?"

"I'm 97. Like 27 for the 70th time. I'm scared of turning 100. It seems so old. How old are you?"

"I don't know."

"Do you age?"

"I don't know." He was shouting over the music now. "I shave." Time moved so slowly for him now that nothing seemed to change.

"So, you're new to this too." She twirled around in front of him with her hands over her head. He did the same. He had never danced before.

She motioned to him to lean down. "I want to bite you."

"Okay." He had no idea why he agreed.

She grabbed his hand and pulled him into the shadows behind one of the massive support pillars, away from a laser light show. The music was softer there but he could feel the beat in the floor and in his chest.

Moira backed him up until he was standing against the smooth, white tiled wall of the platform. She kissed his mouth, his cheek, his ear, his neck. Having fed, she felt warm now. Her breath was hot against his skin and the smell of garbage was replaced by the scent of ripe fruit.

"Hold on." She pressed a button on the bracelet, producing a whooshing sound like someone inhaling after holding his breath for too long. Opening a compartment on the top with a manicured thumbnail, she dropped a ruby-colored capsule into her hand. "Giles hates it when I tear up my wrists so he makes me wear this old thing."

She placed it between her lips. He kissed her and swallowed it.

The music took on a funky beat. Moira turned her back to him, grinding her rear against him. She laced her fingers over his, and ran his hands over her body arching her back.

He looked out and saw colors - Moira's dress was a dark blue and his shirt was a deep red. It dawned on him that they were in the dark and had been since they arrived.

Moira turned and pressed against him. She raked her teeth over his nipple. Even through his shirt, the sensation was penetrated his thoughts. Goosebumps raced across his chest.

"Lean down."

He bent his knees a little to be her height. Stepping between his legs, she reached up and turned his head. It stung when she bit his neck and drank from him, alternating licking and kissing him. Then, the pain dissolved. She scratched her nails across his chest, and then smoothed over the marks.

It was almost like rapture. His body was turning liquid. He relaxed and closed his eyes. "Oh, God" he said.

147

She bit his shoulder hard and shoved him against the wall. His eyes snapped open at the stinging pain. "Would you quit it with the 'Oh, God' shit?" Her upper lip twitched. "Fuck me! You can destroy a mood." She pushed herself away from him.

"It feels like…"

"I know what it feels like." She pulled him close again, untucking his shirt and unbuttoning the top button of his jeans. "It feels like lust."

Toying with the waistband of his boxers against his stomach, she kissed him. The dirty, black ceiling became a velvet sky laced with stars. If he could just pray, he would return to heaven, but his prayers were interrupted by thoughts of possessing her. "Why are you doing this?"

"Look at me," she said. Surprisingly, her eyes were not green but a jumble of tiny flecks of yellow and blue. Her face was dazzling even as he realized it was his blood that reddened her lips. "Do you want me?"

"Yes."

"Drink." She twisted a valve on the bracelet and offered it to him.

As he drank, her hand snaked into his pants and she bit his neck again. With his hands resting on her hips, the blood connected them – mouth and hand – to the same beat, his pulse, as one creature. Weightless and blinded by light, he thought she had killed him until his vision resolved to the cavernous dark of the club. The distant drumbeat of crappy hip-hop returned. His legs felt like lead and he was starving. Straightening up, his back complained so he wrapped his arms around her and braced against the wall.

She had done this before - or tried to - so she should have expected what came next. She should have been able to fend it off emotionally. Instead, when his legs buckled and he slumped against the wall and he whispered "thank you" into her hair, it hurt. High on human blood, she was losing focus. Wrapped in his warm arms, feelings stirred in her despite every attempt to quell them. She could have stood there forever.

Moira wiped her mouth on the back of her hand. "C'mon. Let's feed you."

She led him back to the lab, staring at the slight slope of his broad shoulders, replaying the way his eyes closed and a shudder passed through him. She cursed the conflict pulling at her skin – maybe she should just tell him everything. *This had to happen.* Her moral opposition to the idea of hardening from the moment she was turned and pressed into service working on the Yanks headed to the European Theater in WWI. Joining the underground. Becoming part of this enclave. The years they had wasted with the blood of virgins and do-gooders who might become saints. How Giles had drained nearly half of the Sisters of Loreto in Albania hoping to save Adam's father in 1950.

Back in the lab, the angel wolfed down the best chicken sandwich he had ever tasted.

"I may be a murderess but you, sir, are a fucking thief." Moira watched, incredulous. "All this time in that *fine* body and you never...? Never even wanted to?"

He shook his head, "Sex is a distraction from my work."

"Well, it gets the blood moving. Better than a transfusion."

"Why chicken?" he asked around a mouthful of sandwich.

"It's like any other chicken farm. They can take the dark."

He stopped between bites to sip his coffee, also delicious. He looked at the cup, "What kind of coffee is this?" Even the aroma was alluring.

Moira shrugged. "Some old amp from Columbia brings it in fresh each day." She watched him eat. "That's the blood. It's not so pleasant when it wears off. The blood changes you until it's hard to remember being human."

"Funny," he said. "I'm a vegetarian, suffering and all."

"And I'm a humanitarian. How do you feel?"

"Invincible. I could do anything right now. It's extraordinary."

He stood up, stretched his shoulders, and did a handstand. He lowered himself down until his hair burshed the ground, pressed his arms straight again, and padded around in a circle.

While he was playing, a guard came in and whispered something to Moira but he could hear it clearly.

The angel flipped back onto his feet. "What about Adam?"

"Nothing. Come here," she said. "Take off your shirt."

Modesty had taken hold of him again and, while he came to stand next to her, he turned away to unbutton the borrowed shirt. She helped him slip the shirt off his shoulders and pulled his t-shirt off over his head revealing the long red scars that ran behind his scapula on each side, each as wide as her finger. She kissed them, the enhancements worked both ways. She tried to shake the thought of him.

When he turned, a few traces of her fingernails remained. She reached for the zipper of his pants but he shooed her hand away.

"I can do that myself."

She patted the gurney. He kicked off his shoes, stripped off his pants, and jumped up on the table. She leaned in to kiss him.

He held out his arms as if to embrace the world. " I feel so... OUCH."

Giles, the lab technician, withdrew the needle. *Where had he come from?*

The angel's face tingled and his limbs began to numb. Deftly, Giles tilted the angel onto his back and flipped his legs up onto the gurney. As the paralysis spread, the technician hooked up a set of IVs.

"Why?"

Giles smiled, a broken picket fence of grey teeth. His tongue had been cut out a long time ago.

Moira came to the edge of the gurney, her silky black hair falling in her face. She smoothed his forehead with warm fingers. "The tests work but, since you are no longer fully an angel, we're goin'ta need more blood than we originally thought." She kissed him. "Like, all of it."

Eerily silent, Giles set about attaching an embalming pump to his other arm. With the flip of a switch, cool fluid flowed in while his blood pumped out and collected in a jar. Giles retreated through the doors to the next room.

"Adam is the last remaining living relation I have - my great, great grandson. His parents and his sister were killed in a car crash some years ago. Adam survived but an orphan spotter brought him here for hardening. Giles and I have tried to keep him here as a feeder but he's so strong – wiry strong – and so fast that Sammael would have him be a soldier. I can't hide Adam anymore; I have to save him. He doesn't know."

Moira explained their experiments – the failed transfusions, the dark rituals. She had killed more virgins than Countess Báthory. "Blood Countess, my eye," she said. "You're my only hope – the blood of an angel."

"No one knows mmm..." his mouth disobeyed. "Nuh un..."

"No, no one knows you're here."

The angel woke to find the ever-silent Giles removing the tubes from his arms. Moira uttered something too low for him to hear and the man scurried away into a dark corridor.

Moira leaned over his gurney, a faint hint of her strawberry breath touched his face. He did not feel any pain.

The guard wheeled in another gurney where Adam thrashed against three sets of leather restraints. Giles trailed behind them. Unable to turn his head, the angel watched the action in a surgical mirror.

"You can't do this!" Adam bridged his body, flecks of spit exploding into the air as he shouted. "I won't go back!"

"It's for your own good, pet," Moira cooed. "You can live in the sun, marry, have a family. This is no life for a man."

"I'll kill you for this! I'll kill you!" Adam's wrist and ankles were abraded and bloody.

After struggling to set up an IV, Giles injected something yellow into Adam's arm and it stopped moving. Ever efficiently, Giles hooked up the peristaltic pump and connected Adam to the canister of the blood removed from the angel. The dark red fluid flowed into the child. The soft rhythm of the machine was barely audible under Adam's shouting but, after a few moments, the ability to fight ebbed from him and his threats of homicide were reduced to a babble of "kill you... kill you all." His legs gave way and he flopped down on his back. After a few minutes, he was still.

"Turn off the pump," Moira commanded. About one third of the angel's blood was left in the reservoir.

Confusion seeped into the angel's brain. In the deepening cold, he did the math three times to be sure but he estimated they had taken more than two quarts of his blood. Only his exposure to Moira's blood was keeping him from hypovolemic shock.

So, this was how he was going to die – paralyzed and cold in the silence of an abandoned streetcar station. He was ebbing now. *"How long?"* he wanted to ask.

Afraid that if he closed his eyes he would never open them again, the angel offered a silent prayer of thanksgiving that Adam would live then added, *"And take pity on this, your humble servant... into your hands..."*

As Moira's warm hand drifted down his body, he looked up at the dirt and cobwebs hanging down from white-washed concrete ceiling. Moira's fingers were absently curling the hair on his belly. Darker thoughts took hold of him - *into her hands... in her mouth... inside her. The next time she said, 'Fuck me,' he would. He would pull up her dress and make her cry out with the pleasure or – better – the pain of him. When she cried, 'oh, god,' she would mean him.* As soon as he had the thought, he began a prayer of atonement.

Giles tended to Adam. Vital signs, temperature, even the boy's pale complexion had taken a turn toward human numbers.

"It's better than we ever thought!" Moira said.

"Help me..." From his gurney, Adam stirred slowly and his whimpering noises resolved to speech, "I can't see."

"Let him up," Moira commanded. The guard hesitated. "Do it."

As the guard undid the last restraint, Giles was ready with his needle but he never had the chance to act. Adam moved with superhuman speed twisting Giles into administering the shot to his own leg. The old man collapsed. Spinning, Adam pulled the guard's pistol and shot the man in the stomach. The guard toppled forward into gurney taking it, the IV stand, and the pump over with him. What remained of the angel's blood arced across the floor.

Adam backed away holding the pistol to his head, "I can't live like this again. I can't." With whatever vampire agility remained, he fired two shots into his head.

The gunshots blinded the angel but he could hear Moira saying "No, no, no" punctuated by her enraged scream.

Moira ran to the side table and she climbed on top of him, straddling him. She held out two pre-filled syringes. "One is etorphine – enough to stop a rhino – and the other is the antidote. I think it's narcan. I don't know which is which and Giles is paralyzed. Blink, if…"

For a second, she studied the angel's face for signs of movement, then dropped the syringes. "I'm sorry," she said. "I know why you came here."

Stripping off the antique bracelet, she poured blood into his gaping mouth. Even as sensation and heat raced back into his body, he could not move.

In his borrowed body, he felt the change come. At first, there was a terrible awareness –the speed at which his nails were growing, how loose individual hairs were, the speed and direction of every red blood cell, the awakening twitch of each muscle fiber as Moira's blood overcame the tranquillizer. A deep hunger invaded him, a thousand different appetites to fill but, first, this one.

He sat up and began to feed from her, sucking with the half-closed eyes of a nursing baby.

ABOUT THE AUTHORS

Susan Basso McCauley worked for several years as an actress and English instructor in Los Angeles where she obtained her MFA in writing from the University of Southern California. In 2002, Susan moved to London where she received an MA in Text & Performance. In London, her stage adaptation of Gogol's *The Nose* was produced at Royal Academy of Dramatic Art's George Bernard Shaw Theatre, and scenes from her play *The Prisoner: Princess Elizabeth* were performed at the Tower of London. After returning to the U.S, she was the line producer of the Emmy Award nominated short film *Now and Forever Yours: Letter to an Old Soldier.* She now lives in Houston, Texas with her husband and young son where she teaches for the University of Houston Clear Lake and continues to write. More information is readily available on her website: www.susanbassomccauley.com

CAT is a philosopher queen and coffee achiever whose short stories, essay, and novels often deal with what it is like to be a human, what it means to be good, or what it means to be "a man." She enjoys Scotch whiskey and likes to write in hotel bars – especially when they don't guard their pianos. She has spoken on science, public policy, and writing. In her spare time, she edits science textbooks. She is currently working on a screenplay about dating.

A founding member of the League of Eclectic Authors, **Clint Collins** was previously published in the first anthology of the Horror Writers Association, "Under the Fang," and in other anthologies such as "Lillith Unbound," "Cthulhurotica," and "50 Shades of Decay." He currently lives with his lovely wife Beverly near a lake full of alligators in south central Florida.

George A. Crawford is a retired Air Force officer. He has published two books in the supernatural genre: *Paw,* which was a quarter-finalist in the Amazon Breakthrough Novel Award, and *Soldiers of the Night: Green Berets vs. Vampires*, both of which are available as electronic books through Amazon Kindle. George has also published non-fiction professional military

155

books and numerous articles, and is currently at work on a series of techno thrillers.

Randall Dunn graduated from The Pennsylvania State University with degrees in International Relations, Russian Studies and Russian Language. He served as an Intelligence Officer in the U.S. military; and since 9-11, he has completed several combat deployments to war zones. Mr. Dunn is the author of the international thriller *Rattlesnake Island*; and is currently working on its sequel, *Moscow Nights*. You can learn more about his writing or contact him at his website at www.RNDunn.com.

Daniel Fobes lives and works in the Washington D.C. area. His previous short stories have appeared in numerous magazines since the mid 1990s. Currently, he is working several writing projects including a historical fiction novel.

Walt Gavenda has been a keen student of the paranormal for all of his adult life and is currently investigating Civil War ghosts and haunts for several upcoming projects. He is the co-author of *A Guide to Haunted West Virginia* and frequently lectures on ghosts and the paranormal. Mr. Gavenda currently resides "in my foxhole on the edge of reality" where he wrote this story.

After reading Bradbury's "All in a Summer Day", **Judy Gibson** was so excited that a friend introduced her to the science fiction and fantasy section of her high-school library. Judy was immediately hooked and still reads fantasy to this day. After finishing a computer science degree, she moved to northern Virginia for work and so loved the area that she bought a townhouse in Reston. Judy attended her first meeting of the League of Eclectic Authors because she liked the name; she stays because she likes the people. "Pickpocket", written for the League's anthology, was work-shopped at the Writer's Center in Bethesda and is Judy's first published story. She is currently working on her first novel, a tale of demons and angels, a tale of betrayal and trust.

Donald Jeffries is the author of the 2007 sci-fi/fantasy *The*

Unreals. He has written extensively on a variety of political and social topics, and his book *Hidden History: An Encyclopedia of Modern Crimes, Conspiracies, and Cover-Ups in American Politics* is scheduled for release by Skyhorse Publishing in the fall of 2014.

Robin Masnick graduated Phi Kappa Phi with a B.S. degree in Computer Science and a M.S. degree in Strategic Leadership. As a former Federal Employee, she worked as a computer specialist before accepting the role of Functional Area Manager, leading many critical projects that had direct impact on US national security. After working for the U.S. Coast Guard and DHS FEMA for the past 15 years, she decided to take a sabbatical and pursue her passion for creative writing. Robin lives in the eastern panhandle of West Virginia with her husband, a retired USCG Chief Petty Officer, and can be contacted via her blog http://robinmasnick.wordpress.com/

Clint Mesle is an author, playwright and screenwriter who lives and writes about Northern Virginia. A number of his plays have been produced by The Source Theatre, The Tavern Stage and The Arts Council of Washington, D.C. He is currently working on his second novel and has a number of short stories due to be published in anthologies in 2014.

Lorri Stone is frantically trying to pass for an adult. She is a lifelong Virginian with a husband and two dogs. She has seen the Grand Canyon, ridden a motorcycle, smoked a Cuban cigar, worked at the Pentagon, put up with fibromyalgia, and written a few stories.

Previously published in the online literary magazine Halfway Down the Stairs, **M.B. Wallace** lives in Northern Virginia USA with her wonderful husband and two astonishingly loud schnauzers. She enjoys writing, doing voiceover work, and fantasizing that the Washington Capitals will someday win the Stanley Cup.

Scott Woodward is a former intelligence officer and consultant. He resides in Virginia with his wife, two children, golden retriever, and three cats. His favorite author is H.P. Lovecraft.